Tea Cups and Turning Points

Naina More is a TEDx speaker, celebrated motivational speaker, life coach and certified psychological counsellor, renowned for her powerful voice on mental wellness, confidence and self-growth.

A Chartered Accountant by qualification, she has inspired thousands through her live shows, public speaking sessions and high-profile interviews with over 100 celebrities. Naina has also been honoured with the Femina Women Achiever Award and was featured in *Femina*'s 'Most Powerful Women 2020' list.

Her versatile work spans multiple platforms—as a columnist, poet and media personality—with publications in leading national outlets. Her acclaimed show *Zindagi Aapki Hai* on Taaza TV and Instagram Live addresses real-life issues with empathy and insight.

Passionate about social impact, Naina works with underprivileged communities and regularly engages with youth across India on topics like mental fitness and self-acceptance. As a committed social activist, she works at the grassroots level for the upliftment of marginalized groups.

Balancing her many roles as a mother, mentor and change-maker, Naina is a voice of empowerment in modern India.

You can connect with Naina on:
Instagram: @nainamoreofficial
Facebook: Naina More

Tea Cups and Turning Points

A Collection of Short Stories

Naina More

RUPA

Published by
Rupa Publications India Pvt. Ltd 2025
161-B/4, Gulmohar House,
Yusuf Sarai Community Centre,
New Delhi 110049

Sales centres:
Bengaluru Chennai
Hyderabad Kolkata Mumbai

P-ISBN: 978-93-7003-040-4
E-ISBN: 978-93-7003-602-4

First impression 2025

10 9 8 7 6 5 4 3 2 1

The moral right of the author has been asserted.

Jai Shri Shyam

∽

This book is dedicated to my God, Sai,
and to my husband, Rohit—
each a guiding force in my life
who always sees in me
what I cannot yet see in myself.

Contents

1

Hues of Awakening

The loud sound of *shankha* echoed in my ears, followed by the faint *ulu-dhvani*—ululation—rising from a distant temple. Rickshaws honked along the street with their familiar beep-beep—the sound of old rubber horns still stubbornly intact, resisting replacement by modern electronic ones.

I got up from my bed, folded the blanket and embraced the evening with a fresh body and a clear mind. The strong fragrance of freshly burnt *dhunachi* filled the air, curling into my nostrils. Kaki-ma must have begun *sandhya*—the evening ritual of lighting the diya, offering prayers to Goddess Durga and burning the sacred Bengali incense, *dhuno*.

After completing her prayers, she would walk around every nook and corner of the house with the dhuno burner in hand, letting the smoke push away any lingering negativity. There is something deeply symbolic about Bengali rituals that hold me captive. Whether it's the blowing of the shankha, the ululation or the steady burn of dhuno, each act is designed not just for tradition—but for transformation. A sacred cleansing of the soul and space—sending away what no longer belonged. Grief. Bitterness. Fear.

Before I got married and moved to Kolkata, I was unfamiliar with Bengali culture and its many layered traditions. I had made a sincere effort to read about the city and its people, but no book offers the intimacy that real experience provides. It has been less than a month since I arrived, and yet it feels as if it might take a lifetime to truly understand this city and trace the roots of its heritage.

I touched Kaki-ma's feet as she entered my room. She murmured something in Bengali, a language I was still learning to understand, but her expression was clear. It was a blessing—one that prayed for the long life of my husband. That's how Indian mothers are. Their love flows through the sons they raise and the blessings they bestow on daughters-in-law often revolve around the men they adore—rarely do they say, 'You be happy'. The bride's joy remains an unspoken hope.

Kaki-ma is my husband's aunt, but she's been like a mother to Anurag ever since his parents died in a car accident. He had not even stepped into his teenage years back then. Her own daughter lives in Bombay and rarely visits. After Kaku passed away, it was Anurag who took charge of the house and Kaki-ma.

We haven't had a chance to have a proper conversation with each other. The language barrier is real, but it's more than that. From her gestures, I can make out she doesn't like me very much.

She pointed to the sindoor on my dressing table, motioning for me to apply it. Her brows furrowed as she noticed my long hair flowing freely down my back. Here, it is considered inauspicious to leave your hair open during the peak of the evening. I understood what her silence said. Without argument, I quickly knotted my hair into a bun. She left the room with a quiet nod, seemingly content.

Evenings, for me, meant sitting by the window with a cup of ginger tea in hand and a quiet longing in my heart. A longing for companionship—for someone willing to dive into the ocean of my emotions and swim gently through the symphony of my silences.

From across the street, I could see artisans crafting the idol of Goddess Durga, giving delicate attention to her brows, her sharp nose, her wide-open eyes. The precision mesmerized me. She looked perfect, almost unnervingly so. I found myself wondering—does such perfection truly exist in reality?

Anurag had told me about Durga Puja—just two months away now. He spoke of it with such reverence, describing it as not just a festival but a pulse that ran through every street and soul in Bengal. He said that in those days, the city transformed: new clothes, fresh furniture, decorated homes and a fever of excitement in every heart. Everyone became consumed with preparations, glowing with anticipation.

He had smiled and said, 'We don't bring Maa home just like that. We bring her with pomp and zeal. Each pandal will be a world of its own, each with its own theme and its own beautifully sculpted idol. Even seven days won't be enough to cover all the major ones—forget the smaller ones.'

I was looking forward to it. I wanted to experience every bit of the festival with Anu by my side—his hand in mine, his presence a soft reassurance. I missed him deeply.

Anu wasn't the first man in my life. I had remarried after enduring an abusive marriage at a tender age—an experience that left me disillusioned with the very idea of marriage and with men.

As I sipped my tea and watched the artisans across the street shaping Durga's idol, memories of another time surfaced—of when Anu first entered my life like a monsoon storm, unexpected and unannounced.

Good things often arrive when you least anticipate them.

He had come to Varanasi for an All India Doctors' Summit and was posted under my father's department. During those three days, he worked closely with Papa, soaking in every bit of his knowledge. Papa liked him— perhaps more than he admitted. When the conference ended, Anu checked out of his hotel and left for the airport. Before parting, my father had asked him to stay in touch and send a message once he reached Kolkata.

But fate had other plans. His flight was cancelled

due to heavy rains. When he called my father to ask for hotel recommendations, Papa instead invited him to spend the night at our home. It was closer, safer and it felt like the right thing to do.

Anu resisted at first but eventually agreed, not wanting to get stranded in the storm. That night, we shared an hour-long conversation and I surprised myself—words poured out as if I had been waiting for someone like him to arrive. The next morning, Papa asked me to show him around the city. I hesitated, but something in me wanted to know him more.

I didn't realize how quickly time flew by with him. One conversation led to another, then another. We quickly fell into a rhythm, a quiet understanding that neither of us had anticipated. It wasn't love at first sight—it was trust at first conversation.

Anu was intelligent, handsome, successful—a true gentleman. But more than anything, it was his simplicity that struck me. I used to be a talker, once upon a time, until the shadows of a toxic relationship made silence my armour. I had stopped sharing, retreating inward.

But Anu was a master of stillness. He could go hours without speaking. To fill the silences, I found myself talking again—and for once, it felt safe. In him, I found a listener patient enough to wait until I rediscovered my voice.

One day, midway through lunch, he paused, looked at me and smiled.

'Do you know,' he said, 'you're like a chirpy bird—full of life and melody.'

His words startled me.

I blinked, caught off guard.

'Am I?' I asked, surprised by his observation.

In his company, I was slowly rediscovering myself. The version of me that had been buried beneath years of pain and silence was stirring again, awakening with each passing hour.

We talked endlessly, opening up like two windows in the breeze. He told me about his parents—both gone. He spoke of his aunt, his routines, his city and its culture. With every word, he was letting me in and without realizing it, I was doing the same.

I was enjoying every moment. But I reminded myself, firmly, that I had no intention of falling in love. I had loved once—and been betrayed deeply. That part of me was supposed to be sealed away forever. I had promised myself never to trust a man again.

Though he didn't speak much, his eyes spoke volumes. Sometimes, they lingered on me longer than necessary, not with lust, but with something warmer, more tender. His eyes would brighten whenever I smiled. When I crossed the street, they followed me with unspoken worry.

They made me feel seen in a way I hadn't been in years.

I didn't want him to feel this way. I was just being kind—just being a guide. This was not supposed to mean anything. But his gaze made me feel things I didn't want to feel—discomfort and comfort all wrapped in one.

He wasn't my future. He was a placeholder, a patch

on a torn fabric. This warmth I was feeling? It was just the warmth of being normal again. It had nothing to do with him...or so I told myself.

It was dusk and the day he had to leave had arrived. He asked if I would accompany him to the airport, but I declined. I said it would be too late for me to return home, though the real reason was more complicated—I wanted to put some distance between us.

He nodded but asked if I would at least join him for a cup of tea before he left. I agreed, already planning to finish it quickly and make a quiet exit.

We strolled through a narrow lane towards a small tea stall at the corner. It was the season of rains and the drizzle had begun, soft and scattered. People were retreating from the streets, scurrying home before the heavens opened fully.

We sipped our steaming kulhads while raindrops landed gently on our skin. As the drizzle turned into a steady downpour, Anu suddenly grabbed my hand and tugged me under a nearby shade. For a moment, we stood in silence. Then I looked at him—his hand still firmly holding mine. He caught my gaze but didn't release it. Instead, he squeezed it tighter.

I felt the heat rise in my cheeks. I wanted to pull away, to say something, anything. But before I could, he leaned in and whispered, 'Will you marry me?'

I became numb, frozen, completely at a loss for words. He looked into my eyes, read the chaos in them and gently pulled me closer.

'I think I said the last thing first,' he murmured. 'So

let me say the first thing now… I love you.'

He leaned, slowly, deliberately. His lips hovered near mine. My mind raced—urging me to move, to resist, to flee from the intensity of the moment.

But then there it was, buried deep within: the longing to be loved, to be seen, to be touched without fear.

And so I didn't move.

I responded, with a deeper kiss, letting our mouths explore each other with rising urgency. His touch awakened something long buried—desires I had once locked away in fear. I craved more, all of him, all at once.

And yet, even in that moment of intensity, he remained gentle. A man in control of his emotions, honouring mine.

It wasn't him who lost himself—I did. I was overwhelmed, physically and emotionally, wanting him to touch every curve, to cross every boundary I had drawn.

But he stepped back, drawing a line I wasn't sure I even wanted to exist. He must have mistaken my passion for an answer to his proposal.

I couldn't go on without unveiling my truth—my past, with all its shadows and scars. I told him everything.

But he didn't flinch. 'It doesn't matter to me,' he said simply. 'What matters is my future with you—and yours with me.'

I asked him to take time, to reconsider, to be wise. But his conviction was unwavering. His heart had made its choice. The only hesitation in him was whether I'd be willing to embrace his world—his city, his faith, his culture.

And I said yes.

Because sometimes love doesn't knock. It sweeps you off your feet, and for once you don't resist.

Since marrying Anu, not a single day has passed when I haven't thanked every god I know. He filled my life with a happiness I didn't believe marriage could hold. Everything felt surreal, like I was living a dream.

That evening, dressed in a golden baluchari silk sari with a deep red border, I let the pallu flow free, slipped on golden jhumkas, lined my eyes with kohl and put my hair into a neat bun, adorning it with fresh mogras. The final step was putting sindoor on my forehead and pressing a bindi between my brows.

Kaki-ma knocked at the door, peeking in to check if I needed anything. Her eyes scanned me from head to toe. For the first time, her expression softened and something shifted in her eyes. She stepped forward silently, picked up the kohl from my dressing table and placed a dot behind my right ear. It was a small gesture, but in her language of silence, it meant a lot. It wasn't approval yet—but maybe, just maybe, it was the beginning of acceptance.

Each minute felt like an hour as I waited for Anu. He had asked me to be ready by six for his friend's anniversary party—and now it was half past. He was still nowhere in sight.

I was annoyed, yes, but more than that, I was impatient to show him how I looked. I had imagined his reaction over and over—how his eyes would widen, how his lips might part in surprise, how he'd say something that would make me blush.

My face lit up as soon as I heard the doorbell. I rushed toward the door without a second thought. Kaki-ma, who was almost always expressionless, smiled gently at my excitement.

Anu paused at the threshold. Before stepping in, he gave me a long, deliberate look—his eyes slowly travelling from head to toe.

Embarrassed, I turned and ran into the bedroom. He followed.

This wasn't his usual routine. Most days, he'd first greet Kaki-ma, have a cup of tea, chat about his day, dinner and politics before ever thinking about stepping into our room.

They say Bengali boys are mama's boys and I can vouch for it. Anu shares a bond with Kaki-ma unlike anything I have ever seen. She pampers him like a child and he, in turn, obeys her like one. From oiling his hair to folding his clothes to cooking his favourite maach-bhaat—she allows no interference in the rituals she performs for him. She wears her role like armour, with pride and ownership. Anu, too, listens to her in everything—from personal choices to professional decisions. He once told me there's only one time he ever went against her wishes—when he married me.

Kaki-ma wasn't pleased with Anu's decision to marry a divorcee. She might have eventually accepted that I wasn't the quintessential Bengali bahu she'd imagined for him—but what troubled her most was that her beloved son was marrying someone who wasn't new to wedlock. It bruised her heart and I could feel that wound in her silence.

Anu caught hold of my pallu and drew it close to his face, inhaling softly, theatrically. Then, with a mischievous grin, he said, 'It looks like the moon has landed on Earth,' quoting from a classic Hindi film. 'Shall we skip the party and stay in tonight?'

I gave him a gentle push, pretending to ignore his flirtatious smirk—but my smile gave me away.

He wasn't done.

'Looking at you,' he said, 'I realize just how lucky I am. You're the most beautiful apsara God ever created and sent to fill my life with love. You look...ravishing.'

I blushed.

We stayed in each other's arms for a while, until I finally asked him to freshen up and get ready.

'There's a little problem,' he said.

'What problem?' I asked, puzzled.

He paused, eyeing me with a nervous smile. 'You look...breathtaking. Like the most beautiful bride. You'll steal everyone's attention,' he said with a smile. 'But love...it's a cocktail party. Everyone will be in dresses and trousers. I'm just worried you'll feel out of place.'

His words weren't unkind, but I felt a knot of embarrassment tug at my confidence. Not because I was overdressed—but because I so badly wanted to belong. To be part of his world without sticking out like a sore thumb.

I panicked and rushed to change, already tugging at pleats and jasmine strands, whispering to myself how long it would take. Anu helped unwrap everything—each fold of the sari, each strand of jasmine, each clasp of jewellery. From the wardrobe, he pulled out a pair of jeans and a black off-shoulder top sequinned in silver—the same outfit I'd worn on our first official dinner date.

I hesitated. I hadn't worn anything western since our wedding.

'There's always a first time for everything,' he reassured me.

The transformation took minutes. That's the thing about a western look—it's quick and simple. I untied my bun and let my hair fall loosely over my shoulders. The jhumkas were replaced by pearl studs and the makeup shifted from bright to soft and dewy.

I paused before stepping out in front of Kaki-ma. This wasn't a look she'd approve of easily. But Anu held my hand and led me down the corridor, easing my nervousness. I touched her feet, avoiding eye contact and we left immediately.

His friend's house was stunning—every inch of it reflected a deep love for art and music. I was in awe. Each corner had its own soul: vivid paintings, rustic earthen pottery, delicate terracotta figurines, *kaatha* hangings and musical instruments that ranged from the veena to the harmonium and even vintage trumpets.

It wasn't just decoration. It was expression. Even before meeting the hosts, I had already become a fan of their taste.

Anu introduced me to his friends, Sonika and Subodh. I congratulated them on their anniversary and complimented the aesthetic beauty of their home.

'It's like walking through an art gallery that lives and breathes,' I told them, genuinely enchanted.

Sonika smiled and said, 'We Bengalis are true lovers of art and music. Each of us is born with an eye for beauty and an ear for melody. We value art and we nurture it like a part of our family.'

I nodded in agreement. I was beginning to see that very truth unfold before me, not just in their words but in the atmosphere.

We mingled with the other guests—many of them doctors and quite a few of Anu's college friends.

At one point, Anu came over and asked, 'What shall I get for the lady to drink?'

'Just a cola,' I replied.

He grinned and nudged, 'Come on, it's a cocktail party! Let your hair down a little—drink your heart out.'

I couldn't refuse when he insisted. 'Alright then,' I said with a smile. 'Pour me a glass of red wine.'

He chuckled mischievously.

'Has the lioness lost her appetite?' he teased. 'Your father once told me—half in jest, half in exasperation— about how you and your brother stole his bottle of scotch and got caught gulping it neat.'

'That was a lifetime ago,' I laughed. 'I was just a wild teenager then. Now, I'm a lady.'

'And who said a lady can't enjoy a drink of her choice?' he said, raising an eyebrow with mock formality.

His words, though playful, triggered a deeper memory.

My mind flashed back sharply—to another party, another man.

I saw myself dressed in my favourite black gown with its daring V-neckline, red heels adding fire to my step. I hadn't carried a purse that night. I wanted to move freely, to feel light and uninhibited.

'You look stunning,' I told myself as I admired my reflection in the mirror.

I imagined how Harshit would react upon seeing me. Would he flash me his disarming smile, the one that made my heart skip a beat? We were newly married. I was young, carefree and still believed in the magic of love.

He returned from work on time to pick me up—he was always punctual, almost obsessively so—and gave me a slow, scrutinizing look from head to toe.

'What nonsense are you wearing?' he snapped. 'This dress highlights your cleavage. What image will that create in front of my friends?'

I was stunned.

'There's nothing wrong with my dress,' I said, trying to stay calm. 'It's not revealing anything inappropriate. Why should it give anyone a wrong impression?'

My voice trembled with hurt, but I stood my ground.

He sighed with irritation. 'Explaining things to you is a waste of time. What's done is done. Let's just go.'

The drive to the party was in silence. Once we reached there, we entered and started mingling. As the night deepened and the music got louder, I tried to lose myself in the moment. I just wanted to hold my husband's hand and dance with him.

But I couldn't find him. I stood alone in a room full of strangers, waiting for him to come back and be mine again.

He finally returned—an hour later—with a bunch of his friends and introduced me to them. One of them asked why I didn't have a drink. Before I could open my mouth, Harshit laughed and said, 'Oh, she only accepts drinks from me—not from strangers. That's why she's still empty-handed.'

They teased him, saying he was lucky to have such a devoted wife. I smiled politely—a smile that didn't reach my eyes.

The hostess came over and asked warmly, 'What would you like to drink?'

Again, Harshit answered for me. 'A red wine sangria for the lady,' he said.

I gave him a look, hoping he'd catch the discomfort. He didn't. Or maybe he chose not to.

They say feminism prevails now. It's the buzzword of our time. But I still don't know what it truly means in practice. All I know is that it doesn't exist here. Not in my world.

Harshit handed me the glass—a swirl of wine drowning in floating fruits. But I prefer it strong—60 ml of neat scotch, no ice. The kind that gives me a happy high, not just a social pass.

But strength in women unsettles men like him. We are told we have equal rights—as long as our choices fit within the invisible cage our husbands build. We're allowed to drink, but only what they approve. We can speak—but not too loudly. The man who 'permits' us to be free still holds the reins. Since when do we need permission for freedom?

Marriage is supposed to be a partnership. Isn't it? But too often, it's control dressed as progress. We are expected to smile, behave, nod and call it love. What do you call that? I don't know the perfect word. But perhaps it's hypocrisy.

We left the party sometime after midnight. Harshit was completely drunk—barely able to climb the stairs.

I, perfectly sober, helped him up to the room.

His body sagged against mine like dead weight and yet I carried him—because that's what wives are supposed to do. Isn't it?

'The party was so much fun,' he slurred. 'I'm sure you had a whale of a time, baby.'

I looked at him and asked softly, 'Why did you answer on my behalf all evening? And why did you hand me a glass of wine—when you know I prefer scotch?'

He straightened a little, the smugness returning. 'I have a reputation among my friends,' he said. 'I can't risk spoiling it by letting them see my wife drink scotch.'

I stared at him, stunned. 'What's wrong with it?' I asked.

He didn't flinch. 'Wine is elegant. It's ladylike. It makes a woman look refined. Scotch, on the other hand—it's a man's drink. It speaks of liberty, of power. You women are meant to drink cola and fruit juice. But you should be grateful—we men now allow you to drink alcohol with us. The least you can do is drink modestly and be sober in public.'

I stared at him, disgusted.

'How can a drink define whether a woman is refined or not?' I snapped. 'It's just a matter of personal taste. And who are you to "allow" anything? Women can do what they want—just like men. And so can I.'

His expression twisted. Then, without warning, his palm struck my right cheek.

'How dare you raise your voice at me?' he roared. 'Yes, women can do what they want—but not married women. A wife does what pleases her husband.'

I stood frozen. Shocked. Tears rolled silently down my cheeks. I wanted to hit him back. To scream. To throw something. But before I could act, he collapsed on the bed—passed out cold.

I wept through the night. A strange mix of rage, pain and disbelief churned inside me. By morning, he acted as if nothing had happened. And strangely...I went along with it. I didn't confront him. I don't know why. Maybe I wanted peace more than justice. Maybe I still loved him too much to ignite another fire.

I told myself it was a one-time thing. I promised myself I would not let this happen again.

But it happened again. And again. And again. I didn't realize how gradually I was becoming someone else—someone smaller. I began making every effort just to please him, to keep him happy. He had his own rigid opinions on what women should be. And though I didn't agree with his definition, I still tried to fit that mould. I told myself I had to save our relationship. That love and marriage only happen once and it was my responsibility to make it work. At any cost.

With Harshit, I saw the ugliest side of a man's world—a world where men appointed themselves kings. The irony is that I slowly began to believe maybe this was normal. That all men were like this. That I simply had to adjust, to accept, to endure.

My free-thinking dulled. My opinions shrank. I was becoming a puppet—strings pulled by Harshit's expectations. The arguments I once made in defence of women's rights, of equal footing, all faded into the background. Eventually, he declared himself the winner in every debate about marriage being a partnership. I stopped trying to prove otherwise.

His definition of marriage was disturbingly transactional. Marriage, to him, meant fulfilling three things—physical, emotional and financial needs. The man provides financial support. Offers physical intimacy (which he reminded me he could get elsewhere, but 'chose' to give to me). And in return, the wife? She offers emotional obedience. Silent loyalty. A partner who follows orders, unquestioningly.

The clinking of glasses brought me back to the present. Anurag was standing in front of me, holding two glasses of scotch.

He raised a toast and murmured, 'Cheers to us—and to the good life ahead.'

We drank.

Then another round. And another. And when

dessert arrived, he lit up like a child at the sight of the rosogullas.

I laughed and stopped him. 'You'll get too high. No one eats sweets after drinks—it'll shoot your sugar and your spirits!'

'Why shouldn't you or I be high?' Anu grinned. 'It's a party—let's just have fun.'

He grabbed my hand and pulled me on to the dance floor. We danced without care, tangled in each other's arms, swaying with laughter and rhythm. The night shimmered with joy and, for once, I wanted time to pause.

Later, we returned to the buffet, but I was too tired from dancing to eat. Anu, refusing to let me skip dinner, scooped up a bite and gently fed me. 'With us, you'll learn to eat,' he said. 'Because nothing—not even time— can keep a Bengali away from biryani. We can eat it with our eyes closed and our hands tied.'

Everyone around us burst into laughter—and I laughed too. It was already past midnight, but his friends showed no signs of winding down. They were deep into debates about sports and politics, their voices animated and passionate. They were thrilled to have someone 'non-Bengali' in their circle—me. And I, unexpectedly, became their mirror—someone to whom they could explain the beauty, quirks and pride of being Bengali.

Everyone loves their roots, I'm sure. But Bengalis take it to another level. They're unabashedly proud of their language, their traditions and, most of all, their intellect. Every Bengali I met that night had an opinion about something—especially politics. They read about it, debated it, analysed it. And each of them had a personal take, sharpened like a fine tool.

Anu and his friends told me Kolkata was once famously known for its 'Three M's'—Marxism, Mishti and Mother Teresa. Then they asked if I had taken a boat ride along the Hooghly River yet.

I shook my head and their eyes widened in mock horror.

'You're missing out on something truly magical,' they said.

And I believed them.

A few of his friends' wives let me in on a secret. 'If you want to keep a Bengali man happy,' one of them whispered, 'just feed him maach-bhaat—fish and rice. It works every time.'

I couldn't stop giggling.

I also learnt the meaning of the golden word Anu uses all the time—'lyadh'. If I ask him to watch a movie, he says he's feeling lyadh. Ask him to shower or go shopping and he'll sigh, 'Uff, lyadh.' I'd been wondering what this mysterious word meant for the longest time and finally, one of his friends revealed the big secret.

'Lyadh means lazy,' he said, laughing.

By then, I'd already accepted that everything is 'eaten' in Bengal. They eat water. They eat cigarettes. They even eat tea. It no longer shocked me. In fact, I found it endearing.

I smiled to myself as we drove home, leaning back in my seat.

'Play something romantic,' I said to Anu.

He obliged. Rabindrasangeet filled the car.

'It's unbelievable,' I said. 'Tagore can be everything—but romantic? Really? I thought he was more about nostalgia, motivation and humanitarian ideals.'

'What are you saying?' he objected gently. 'How can the great Rabindranath Tagore's music not sound romantic to anyone?'

I felt embarrassed. 'You're right,' I admitted softly. 'I don't know much about Rabindrasangeet. The only two I can name are "Jana Gana Mana" and "Ekla Cholo Re".'

I realized, too late, that I had touched something sacred—one of his emotional chords. Music, especially Tagore's, wasn't just melody to Anu—it was identity. To make amends, I replayed the song.

He looked at me tenderly and began to hum along, then translated the lyrics for me, line by line. 'Aami tomaro shonge bedhechhi amaro praan,' he whispered. 'It means, "My soul has tied its knots with yours."'

I rested my head on his chest, letting the words and rhythm flow through me. There was something magical about the moment—about the way the music merged with the man and the meaning folded into silence.

Once home, Anu locked the door to our room and pulled me close. He kissed me—slowly, gently—starting from the corners of my eyes, tracing down to my lips. I closed my eyes, savouring his touch. But my mind was somewhere else. Still entangled in the past.

Despite all the joy I had felt that night, the ugly memories refused to fade. With my eyes shut, I saw the same party—but with different people. Plastic smiles.

Polished conversation. Men and women sipping drinks with delicate grace, even when too drunk to hold their cutlery properly.

Conversations about swapping partners, endless chatter about the latest exhibitions and newly opened nightclubs. Critiquing strangers' dance moves, dissecting private lives.

I was there—but I never belonged. I took part in those nights with Harshit—the post-party experiments, the reckless intimacy. But none of it touched me. I was present, but not alive. It was duty, not desire. Routine, not passion. I was simply performing the role of an obedient wife.

A single tear fell on Anu's chest. He stopped immediately. Gently, he wiped my cheeks.

He looked at me and asked, 'Can you keep your eyes open for a few more hours?'

I nodded.

We stepped into the car. The next thing I remember, we were on a boat, drifting slowly down the Ganges.

It was exactly five in the morning. The sun was rising, washing the sky in hues I had no name for. The boat moved gently with the current, swaying like a cradle. Above us, the mighty Howrah Bridge loomed. I looked up and felt small—but safely so. We floated to the middle of the river. From that distance, the ghat looked like a painting—lined with wildflowers and trees. I dipped my hand into the water and felt the cool brush of tiny fish.

The breeze kissed our faces. As strands of my hair

danced across my cheeks, my soul, finally, felt at peace. I wanted to stay in that moment forever.

Anu took my hand. I smiled.

'Why did you bring me here?'

He looked towards the horizon. 'I didn't know how else to help,' he said. 'Sometimes I'm afraid I'll never fully understand the pain you carry. I want to fix things— but I don't always know how.'

I reached for his hand. For once, I didn't need strength from him—just his presence.

Something shifted inside me. The wind carried away the weight I had dragged for years—the weight of shame, silence and someone else's version of love.

He didn't ask me any questions; he simply said, 'Make peace with whatever has happened in your past. This is a new morning. A new beginning'.

For the first time, I believed it. I wasn't broken. I wasn't unworthy. I was simply human—and finally, free.

I turned to him, my smile slow but sure. I allowed my heart to accept what my mind had only just come to understand: 'No. All men are not like that.'

2

Between Us

'Finally, it is happening!' Shobhit shouted, jumping in excitement.

Nitya, ever composed, remained calm and carried on with her household chores.

Shobhit wrapped his arms around her waist from behind, squeezing her in a tight hug, and said, 'I can't believe it, my dear—our second child will be born in India—our homeland, our love.'

Nitya was, of course, delighted inside. She had never imagined Shobhit's long-pending leave request would actually be approved and that they would soon be flying to India.

It had been five years since they had moved to Dubai. Theirs had been a simple arranged marriage, but who would have thought it would blossom into a love so deep and strong, transcending all boundaries!

As Shobhit left for the office, Nitya's mind drifted into a flashback.

They had first met through a setup arranged by their parents. Shobhit had come to see her at Anand, a famous South Indian restaurant, accompanied by his army of relatives and friends. In India, South Indian joints were a safe bet for such meetings; the cuisine was universally accepted by people across backgrounds. But her father had an entirely different reasoning. He often said, 'Dosas and idlis are cheap everywhere, and if we don't like the boy, at least we haven't spent too much feeding them.'

The usual procedure followed. Nitya greeted each of Shobhit's relatives with folded hands—his dadi, amma, kaki, tai, baba, tau, chacha, bhaiji, didi, jijaji, buaji and bhaiya-bhabhi. As she contemplated whether she should touch their feet, another wave of family members approached—this time from his maternal side: mosi, mosa, mama, mami and nanaji. She promptly dropped her idea of bending down and stuck to a respectful namaste.

She was sure her father would have a heart attack if either she or the boy rejected the match, because he'd have to pay the bill for feeding such a massive crowd. Her eyes scanned the restaurant, searching for Shobhit, but he was nowhere in sight.

His family, however, was courteous and asked her general questions about her hobbies and future plans. They all seemed very cultured and spoke with warmth, putting her at ease. Shobhit's father explained that since Shobhit was the youngest and most cherished member of their family, everyone was excited for his marriage and had wanted to see the prospective bride. Though they were embarrassed by their sheer number, each one had been eager to be part of this moment. They had already liked Nitya based on her pictures, and now her simplicity and quiet grace had won their hearts. He also made it clear that, regardless of how things turned out, they would be footing the bill. Gone were the days when the girl's family had to feel submissive and bear all expenses.

Then three young men joined the table. Nitya recognized Shobhit from his pictures, but he looked even more handsome in person. He wore a crisp white shirt and blue jeans—a timeless combination, and her personal favourite. She wished she could have worn the same; she'd have looked ten times more beautiful and would have been a hundred times more at ease.

She noticed Shobhit stealing glances at her from the corner of his eye and looked away, feeling shy. Soon, the two of them were asked to sit at a separate table to talk and get to know each other. Shobhit, like a true gentleman, pulled out a chair for her, a gesture that did not go unnoticed. She also observed the way he respectfully called the waiter. Ever since *Munna Bhai MBBS* came out, most Indian girls had started judging boys by how they treated waiters. That had become an unspoken criterion. Nitya smiled inwardly, realizing she was indeed one of those girls.

Shobhit asked her to order. She picked her

favourite—masala chai—and he ordered the same. Their conversation began. And then it flowed. Word after word, thought after thought, everything felt effortless. There was an undeniable rhythm between them. Nitya could hardly believe her luck—she had found someone who felt not only like a potential partner but a true friend, a soulmate.

Shobhit told her he had fallen for her the moment he saw her—her eyes, her energy, her presence. Nitya felt the same way, though she didn't say it aloud. Hidden from the rest of the world, beneath the table, he gently held her hand. She was surprised, moved and deeply touched.

Squeezing her hand lightly, he asked, 'Are you ready for a lifelong journey of love with me?'

She giggled almost girlishly and teased, 'What can you do for me?'

'I can leave the world,' he replied, gazing deeply into her eyes.

In that moment, she knew—he was the one.

ఌ

They were still basking in the warmth of their honeymoon phase when a letter arrived.

Shobhit's office had offered him a new role—head of the Dubai branch. Everyone around them, including Shobhit, declared that Nitya had brought him luck. Barely two months into their marriage and he was being sent abroad.

It felt like a dream. With excitement, joy, fear and hope tangled together, they relocated to the Emirates. It was all so alien at first—so different from India. Their first week was spent in Sharjah.

Each morning, Shobhit would leave for his office in Dubai at the crack of dawn and return late at night. Living costs in Dubai were staggering, while Sharjah was far more affordable—hence the company's decision to place them there initially.

Those were among the gloomiest days of their lives. The daily commute took hours; peak hour congestion was dreadful and taxi fares were outrageously high. Nitya often thought that if anyone wanted to bless and curse another person at the same time, they should say, 'May you get the best flat in Sharjah and may your office be in Dubai!'

After a week of constant emails and requests to the company, their prayers were answered—they were finally moved to Dubai.

Dubai glittered with lights and luxury. From the towering Burj Khalifa to the sky-touching buildings across the city, everything shone brightly. Nitya was mesmerized. The Emirates, rich in oil, thrived not just on petroleum but on tourism too. People from all over the world came here, drawn by the allure of fine dining, architectural marvels, thrilling adventures, luxurious malls and unforgettable experiences.

What amazed her most was the fact that one had to buy drinking water. Whether shopping in a mall or walking along a bustling street, if thirst struck, one had to hunt for a supermarket. There was no provision for free drinking water anywhere.

So simple, she mused. *Spend to quench your thirst.* It reminded her how carelessly water was wasted in India, taken for granted and never truly valued.

ꞔ

Sitting with Shobhit in front of the Burj Khalifa, holding hands while sharing Thai coconut ice cream, Nitya relished the view in front of her as a fountain show began, the water dancing beautifully to Arabian music. The place carried a unique vibe.

'Do you think we'll be able to do this?' she asked him softly.

'What?' he asked.

'Make a home in this city. For ourselves?'

'You are my home,' he replied.

That very conversation made everything perfect—a moment to treasure.

Then, suddenly, Shobhit took out his phone, glanced at it, stood up and walked away. Nitya knew instantly. His addiction was calling.

The next day, they went house hunting. Every cab they took was driven by someone from Pakistan, Bangladesh or India. In a foreign land, even someone from Pakistan felt strangely familiar. There was a shared look, a shared sound in the accent, a shared manner of speaking—an unspoken connection. Nitya thought, *We aren't divided by borders, but by politics and its custodians.*

The drivers took them to housing clusters named after countries. They saw buildings labelled India, China, Russia, Emirates and New Zealand. For a moment, Nitya chuckled—travelling from India to New Zealand in just ten minutes. Her amusement faded quickly upon seeing 15–20 people crammed into a single room. For them, 'home' meant a mattress among rows of others. A landlord explained that the buildings had been designated for Russians, but when they didn't come, the rooms were given to bachelors from India, Pakistan, Bangladesh, the Philippines and Sri Lanka.

Eventually, after much searching, Nitya and Shobhit found a small studio apartment—just a single room, but beautiful and affordable. It was perfect.

Their first day there felt like stepping into a dream. Raised and married into a joint family, Nitya had always dreamt of a space where she ruled—queen of her own home. The hustle began. While Shobhit adjusted to his new workplace, Nitya adjusted to a new lifestyle. House help—commonplace in India—was a rare luxury in Dubai. Here, she had to do everything herself—from washing dishes to cooking meals. It made her long for that morning bed tea prepared and served by someone else—just once.

After a whirlwind week, the weekend finally arrived. Shobhit surprised Nitya with wine, food, rose petals and scented candles. His intent was clear, and she blushed. Amidst the wedding rituals, the gentle hesitations of an arranged beginning and the storm of preparing for life abroad, some things were simply left for later—tender, hopeful but untouched.

They settled into bed, surrounded by fluffy cushions and a plate of fries, watching *Maine Pyaar Kiya* on TV. Back in India, Nitya had always preferred Hollywood movies; she found Bollywood overly dramatic. But here in Dubai, Bollywood felt like home.

Suddenly, Shobhit stood up. 'I'll be back in a minute,' he said.

Nitya stared after him in disbelief. Her heart sank— she was certain it was his addiction dragging him away again. Fifteen minutes passed before he returned with a small packet in his hands. He looked tired, slightly amused and guilty all at once.

'I'm sorry,' he said sheepishly. 'I just didn't want to risk unprotected sex.' He held up the pack of condoms and added, 'Can you believe this? A pack of condoms cost AED 97—₹2,000 for this!'

'Why so?' Nitya asked, surprised.

He explained that the government encouraged Emiratis to have large families. 'They offer financial support, so contraception isn't exactly promoted. Emirati wives are expected to do just one thing—bear as many children as possible,' he said.

Nitya laughed. 'Then next time we go to India,' she said, 'let's bring back more packs of condoms than papads.'

As the strains of 'Mere Rang Mein Rangne Wali' filled the room, they leaned toward each other, lips inching closer.

Nitya suddenly pulled away.

A wisp of stale smoke lingered. The scent of tobacco caught her off guard and something within recoiled.

She turned away quickly, forcing a smile.

Shobhit, interpreting her hesitation as new-bride coyness, smiled back.

But later that night, as she lay curled up in his arms after making love, her thoughts were anything but at ease. The smoke. She told herself not to ruin it. Everything else was perfect.

She had to tuck it away.

෴

Days slipped into weeks. Then five whole years.

She couldn't bring herself to ask him to quit smoking. He had built a world for her in a foreign land. She didn't want to chip at its beauty with a request that felt selfish, even if it wasn't.

Their marriage bloomed. They laughed together, held hands and built a life of memories. They were more like best friends—always joking, always in tune. To everyone who knew them, they seemed the ideal couple. Yet beneath the laughter and love, a quiet disappointment lingered in Nitya's heart.

Nitya often wondered how fast the years had flown by. She took out a pen and paper to make a list of gifts to take home—dates for chachi, perfumes for di, kesar for dadu and a gold chain for maa. She carefully made a detailed note of what to get for everyone.

That evening, rain began to fall—a rarity in Dubai. The world looked transformed. Trees swayed as if celebrating, quenching their long-drawn thirst. The scent of wet earth rose like an aroma of love. Flowers rejoiced under the delicate droplets and the grass glistened, soft and serene.

But rainy evenings often brought a sense of emptiness. Nitya brewed a cup of Arabic tea to fill her void.

'Mama, where are the muddy puddles in rain? I saw them in *Peppa Pig*,' said Sonit, running towards her.

She smiled. 'Where do we find muddy puddles in this land of sand?'

Suddenly, the house echoed with a powerful chant— 'Om bhur bhuva swaha'. Shobhit was home.

As soon as he had freshened up, he emerged and enthusiastically called out, 'Anyone up for some yummy ice cream in this rain?'

Sonit jumped and squealed with joy, 'You are the world's best papa!'

They returned home happily after their ice cream outing. With Shobhit holding her hand, little Sonit by her side and a new life growing in her womb, Nitya felt utterly complete in that moment. They stood on their small, hanging balcony—her favourite spot in the apartment. It was here that romance lingered in the air as the city pulsed below like a living river.

Her heart longed for his full lips; those intense eyes seemed to pierce through her. She drew him towards her with a look and he leaned in, his lips slightly parted. Her heart skipped a beat, her knees turned weak, her eyes fluttered shut—

And then she paused.

Something—old memory, instinct, fear—held her still.

She opened her eyes. He was gone.

The ache returned—a familiar hollowness pressing against her chest. Was it his addiction? Or her silence?

A thousand questions swirled in her mind. She felt her anger rising, tears welling. She turned inward, questioning not just Shobhit, but the divine as well. Was there anyone in God's great ledger who had it all? Or was the Almighty more like an IT specialist—needed only because of life's flaws, its glitches?

The doorbell rang, but even the sacred Gayatri Mantra echoing faintly could not soothe her this time. She got up quickly, blinking away tears and rushed to the washroom to compose herself. But the floor was, and her foot slipped.

The world came to a standstill.

She lost consciousness.

⌀

'She has lost a lot of blood, but we are trying our best to save them both,' said the doctor.

Shobhit moved like a man possessed—running between doctors, surgeons and medical stores. He was numb, emotionless, moving like a machine, trying everything possible to save the queen of his household, of his heart.

Then he saw Maa approaching. He collapsed into her arms, hugging her like a child.

'Baba is home with Shonit,' she informed him. 'I came for you. Everything will be fine. God is kind.'

Then, handing him a creased piece of paper, she added, 'Shonit found this on Nitya's bed. It's signed by her. Might be important—you should read it.'

Shobhit, trembling, unfolded the letter and collapsed into a nearby chair. Yes, it was written by Nitya—his Nitya. He kissed the paper before reading it.

Dear Shobhit,

Tears are rolling down my cheeks as I write this. Today was perfect, my love. I felt so complete. As I place my hand on my belly now and feel this new life blossoming inside me, I am reminded of how many months we spent choosing the perfect name for our son—Shonit. Shobhit + Nitya—your equation, your euphoria.

But this time, I clearly win. Shoniya is waiting to enter our lives and give it even more meaning.

It wasn't child's play to make a home for us in this distant land where we knew no one. It was our partnership, our compassion and our refusal to give up on each other that kept us going. Today, having crossed each hurdle, we have more than just a home—we have a family.

People often say they don't remember the exact moment they fell in love. But I remember mine. It was when you said, 'I can leave the world for you.' But I never wanted you to leave the world. I vowed to stand before you, even in the face of death.

My heart aches knowing that you couldn't leave your addiction for me. What others might dismiss as trivial felt sacred to me. Your promise was sacred—the very foundation of our love. And when you didn't uphold it, it felt like a betrayal.

Time and again, I felt abandoned—not in grand betrayals, but in the little moments. When your hand should've reached for mine, but found a cigarette instead. It breaks my heart to think about those moments when I felt so close to you—only to be forsaken.

Who would believe that a couple so 'perfect' has never even shared a single kiss?

I have imagined it a thousand times. The romance novels I read as a young girl spoke of kisses that could break spells, awaken princesses, make spring flowers bloom... The soft rise on the toes, the head tilt, the passion.

I read about French kisses and Eskimo kisses; I watched Hollywood films where two lips meet with urgency. But I experienced none of them. Not one.

Because you couldn't quit smoking. And I couldn't bear the smell.

You reached for cigarettes when emotion surged, but I craved to taste that emotion on your lips.

Today, for once, you didn't smoke. Your breath was fresh—balsamic, clean. Your sultry mouth drew me in. I thought, this is it. The moment. I am finally going to experience my first kiss.

I felt everything all at once—excitement, tenderness, joy, vulnerability, love, fear. Every nerve in my body was alive. Our lips moved close. It was about to happen.

But something held you back. Or maybe something in me had already pulled away.

It was so hard to gather myself after that, Shobhit. Will you ever realize my pain?

I can't stop crying. I don't know how to regain control of my emotions. I feel weak, betrayed, undesirable, frustrated, incomplete.

But I will never be able to tell you this.

I have written this letter many times before, and each time, I've folded it away, lacking the courage to give it to you.

I never will. My heart understands love. It understands sacrifice.

'Har kisi ko mukammal jahan nahi milta...kahin zameen toh kahin aasman nahi milta.'

Not everyone gets a perfect world...Some don't get the earth. Some don't get the sky.

—Nitya

Her signature was smudged with her tears.

Shobhit sat frozen—like a statue carved in grief. He couldn't move, couldn't speak. His mind spiralled, crashing against wave after wave of memory and regret. He had never realized the depth of her longing.

Before he could process what he had read, the doctor returned.

'I'm very sorry, Mr Kaushik. We couldn't save your child. Your wife is in critical condition. We are preparing for emergency surgery. It's a matter of life and death.'

Shobhit fell to his knees and howled, 'No, Doctor! Please save my wife. I can't live without her—I will die!'

Without waiting, he ran towards the operation theatre, the letter still clutched tightly in his trembling hand.

Inside, doctors and nurses were preparing for surgery. Nitya lay on the cot, draped in wires and tubes. Her body was pale, her lips dry, her face wan and drawn with suffering. But her eyes were open. A single tear rolled slowly down her cheek.

She was still conscious.

Shobhit stepped closer, knowing he couldn't waste this moment. With a heart full of love and eyes overflowing with tears, he bent down and kissed her.

He kissed her like she was oxygen and he, a man drowning.

Nitya kissed him back—with her eyes.

They had their first kiss. A soul kiss.

'This won't be our last kiss,' he vowed. 'I promise—I would leave the world for you.'

And in that moment, Nitya knew she would live.

Just like when the prince kissed Snow White and broke the spell.

That quiet vow had the power to shift everything between them.

3

Destiny, as You May Call

Opening a box of sweets they said, 'We want to take her soon.' My ears were leaned against the back of the door, and hearing this, I jumped in joy.

'*Rishta pakka ho gaya hamari beti ka*—our daughter's marriage has been fixed,' said my father with an expression I could neither read nor describe.

'She is over twenty now, but lucky enough to get a nice boy in one go,' exclaimed my mother.

We were a little below middle class, as one would say. Ours was a difficult family to describe financially. I had four siblings—my elder sister already married, a brother just slightly older than me, and two younger brothers. Life had never been cruel to us, but it had never been generous either. We floated—between feast and famine, hope and heartbreak.

My father, throughout his life, had tried his hands at new business ventures. Someday he would be a partner to someone and sell whitening creams door to door. Those creams, being the new trend in the market, would fill his pockets with handsome money. Those were the happy, rosy days—when we children felt no less than privileged, with decent food to eat, good clothes to wear, and the delight of visiting local fairs, sitting on rides and sharing a plate of aloo chaat. But once the product picked up in the market, competition followed like shadow, and my father would have to give up the business and start over. That would be the time when meals became scarce, and we sometimes went to bed on empty stomachs, our dreams gnawed by hunger.

Yet one thing never changed—our self-respect. We were known as a good family, and each one of us took great care to uphold that reputation. People always looked up to my father as a hardworking, honest man. His shirts were faded, but his name was spotless.

୬

When my elder sister got married, she was fortunate. Her groom was kind, gentle, and earning well as an insurance agent. My father had saved for years for her dowry. Everything seemed perfect.

The groom's family insisted on handling the wedding arrangements, provided we paid them the full amount in advance. We agreed.

The wedding day looked like something out of a

dream. Lights glimmered like stars had fallen from the sky. My sister looked radiant in her heavy red lehenga. Everything they arranged was beautiful—at least on the surface.

Just before the *pheras*, I saw my parents huddled in conversation with the groom's family. Their faces were tight, strained.

'They asked for more money,' my father told me later that night. 'They said the decorations, the venue, the clothes—everything cost far more than what we gave.'

He had no choice. He couldn't stop the wedding. He gave them everything—everything he had saved for both daughters.

I hugged him, my heart heavy. 'The boy doesn't matter,' he said quietly. 'The family does.'

Something cracked inside me then. I promised myself, if ever I got married, my father would not have to go through that pain again.

இ

When the proposal came for me, I watched my parents closely. They seemed calmer this time. Hopeful. The boy's family had not demanded anything. There was no talk of dowry, no hints, no tension.

The minute I saw him, I fell head over heels. He looked handsome as a hero. His presence reminded me of someone who held a high post—perhaps a viceroy I'd seen in old Hollywood movies. His face was expressive, his words captivating. His deep brown eyes could never go unnoticed, and the modesty in his actions would make anyone feel at ease.

He had come to see me with his family—his parents, an elder brother, and a younger sister. 'Amit beta, sit here,' his mother said, placing him across from me.

My heart leapt. That was the first time I heard the name. Amit. It rang in my ears like an echo—the hero of a story I'd always known but never met.

They were stinking rich—the most renowned in their town. His mother wore a perfectly crisp, shimmering sea-green Banarasi sari. His father came in a coat-suit. The elder brother was quiet, but the sister was chirpy.

Amit wasn't shy. He asked about my hobbies, whether I liked cooking.

I nodded. My mother cut in proudly, saying that I not only cooked, but also made the most delicious meals.

Amit lit up and turned to his sister, 'So, finally we'll get *haath ka bana khana* sometimes!'

His mother looked slightly uneasy. 'We have cooks,' she said. 'All we want is for her to bring more smiles into the house.'

They asked, 'Why is your name Durga? You're so soft-spoken.'

I smiled. My sister explained, 'She was born during Navratri. But she always wanted to be called Shalini.'

'Shalini,' they repeated. 'Nice name.'

Later that evening, my mother said, 'The boy liked you very much.'

I smiled shyly and asked, 'He's the one who asked about my cooking, right?'

'They all liked you,' she said, folding clothes. 'Such a good family.'

∽

Wedding preparations began in full swing. Cards were printed and sweets distributed. I didn't even see my wedding card. I was scared to read our names together, afraid of putting an evil eye on the happiness.

'Aren't you going to open one?' my sister teased, waving a sealed envelope.

'No. Let me be surprised at least once in life,' I laughed, tucking it away. But it wasn't truly a joke. I didn't want to do anything that might crack the dream I had begun to live in. I was superstitious. And terrified.

My father looked tired during the preparations—not unhappy, but distant. Once, I caught him watching as I stitched a ribbon on to my trousseau box. I had written, 'Durga loves Amit'. His eyes lingered too long on it.

'Something wrong, Papa?' I asked.

'No, beta. Nothing,' he replied. 'You're happy, no?'

'Very,' I smiled.

He patted my head gently. For the rest of the evening, he avoided my gaze.

∽

One evening, Amit's father called mine. He asked if we could go out together before the wedding. My father hesitated, but he was assured that Sumit, Amit and Gudiya all would be there, and I could be accompanied by my sister.

I called my sister at once. 'Bring your best suit,' I said. 'I want to look...unforgettable.'

Before leaving, my mother pulled me aside. 'Don't talk too much,' she said. 'And never be alone with anyone. Relationships are delicate. Words can ruin things before they begin.'

I promised.

We reached the park on time. Amit looked boyish and smart in his white shirt and jeans.

Gudiya squealed, 'Bhabhi, you're glowing! Pink suits you, doesn't it, bhaiya?'

Both brothers nodded. I blushed.

We all talked. Sumit remained quiet. I ordered an orange ice stick.

Amit laughed. 'You and Sumit both like orange? Who picks orange over Choco Bar?'

I laughed as well.

Then Gudiya and my sister whispered to each other, plotting some mischief. 'Let the couple talk alone,' Gudiya suggested boldly.

My heart raced. But I remembered Maa's words.

'It's getting late,' I said quickly. 'We should go.'

Amit smiled. 'Take care,' he told me.

I held on to that.

Today was 'The Day.' Everyone was busy and happy—except my father. He didn't look unhappy, but his face was blank. After what had happened during my sister's wedding, he must be scared. My mother looked tense. She had promised to offer ladoos to all gods if everything went smoothly.

And yes, everything did go smoothly. In fact, better than I had imagined. The wedding was like a fairy tale. Amit—my Amit—stood beside me in a golden sherwani. His *sehra* was long, the curtain of flowers so thick I couldn't see his face. But I didn't need to. I knew the face behind it. I had already memorized it.

The entire family shimmered in gold—his mother in her signature Banarasi sari, his father regal in a gentleman's coat-suit with golden *safa*, Gudiya glowing in her lehenga. They looked like royalty.

I didn't see Sumit anywhere. Perhaps he was greeting guests, or managing things behind the scenes. I didn't think much of it.

I'll find a beautiful bride for my shy brother-in-law, I thought to myself, chuckling quietly.

We took the seven vows. My hand rested in his. I waited for him to squeeze it, just once, to silently say, 'I'm here'. But he didn't. Maybe he was nervous, overwhelmed. Even the boldest hearts grow quiet during pheras. I smiled to myself.

෴

During the vidaai, I clung to my mother. Then I hugged my siblings. My father—my strong, stoic father—cried like a child. I had never seen him cry like that.

My father-in-law assured him, 'She will be our daughter now.'

I stepped inside the car, my husband beside me. The flowers on the bonnet waved like blessings in the wind.

As the car screeched to a halt outside my new home, someone opened the door and grinned at me. 'Welcome to our family, bhabhi. Can I call you "Shalini bhabhi"?'

It was Amit.

My breath caught. My body froze. The world tilted. Who was beside me?

I stepped out of the car.

I was led inside—my feet dragging, my chest heaving. Gudiya held my hand and whispered warm things I couldn't hear. My mother-in-law stood at the door with a silver plate in hand, diya flickering gently. The women around her sang welcome songs as if nothing in the world had cracked.

Then came the moment. The groom was asked to lift his sehra for the aarti.

He did.

'Sumit,' I whispered.

My body turned hollow. I fainted.

I opened my eyes to a room that wasn't mine. Gold trimmings on the walls. Marigold strands still fresh in the corners. Sumit lay beside me.

He didn't move. Not when I turned. Not when I tried to sit up. He just lay there, flat on his back, eyes fixed on the ceiling fan as if it held the answer to everything.

I looked at him closely. His hands were folded on his

stomach. He was humming, softly. No tune. Just a sound. He flinched slightly when the sheet brushed his wrist, then slowly smoothed it down. Again. And again. And again. Each motion exact, as if wrinkles were a personal insult.

I whispered his name—barely. He didn't turn.

He began tapping his fingers on his palm. A rhythm. Not nervous. Just...practiced.

A sound escaped my throat. It wasn't a word.

What was this? Who was this?

Aunty's words echoed from the haldi ceremony. 'The elder one? Poor thing. The gods gave him something else.'

I had let it pass.

Now, it didn't pass.

Now, it sat in the pit of my stomach and curdled.

I couldn't breathe.

I wasn't in a bridal suite. I was in a room with a stranger. A man who didn't know how to look at me, or speak to me, or even exist beside me.

This wasn't a misunderstanding. This was something else entirely.

I pressed my palms to my eyes. My head pulsed. My chest felt tight.

What had they done? What had I walked into?

꩜

Next morning, I looked pale, eyes swollen. My sister-in-law knocked softly. 'Your brother is here to take you home for the ritual visit.'

I stepped into his arms and cried.

'Don't cry, beta,' my mother-in-law said. 'You'll fall sick.'

My father-in-law sipped his tea, eyes on the newspaper. 'Every girl must adjust. It's only a matter of time.'

Amit came to say goodbye.

He smiled.

I didn't smile back.

When I reached home, everyone rushed forward. They were smiling, laughing, competing to hug me first.

I couldn't respond.

My sister asked, 'Why do you look so serious? You're a bride now, not a widow.'

I broke. 'They tricked us,' I said. 'They finished my life. They trapped me into marrying Sumit.'

Silence followed.

'What made you think you were marrying Amit?' my mother asked gently.

'He was the one who talked to me,' I said. 'He asked about my dreams. He smiled at me.'

'Sumit is shy,' she replied. 'Amit was speaking on his behalf.'

I found my father.

'You knew,' I said. 'You saw me write his name.'

He nodded. 'I saw. But I thought...if you believed you were happy...'

He didn't finish.

And I couldn't say anything else.

I locked myself in my room and lay on the cold marble floor, staring up at the ceiling as if it held the answers I hadn't been allowed to ask. Life around me carried on—cups clinked, someone laughed in the kitchen, and the wind rustled through a half-open window. But inside me, something had gone still.

Not silent in the peaceful sense. Silent like an emptied room. Silent like something sacred had just slipped away unnoticed.

It wasn't just the groom who had been switched. It wasn't just the wedding that had gone wrong. Something else had happened—something that had always been waiting to happen. I had simply never seen it.

No one had lied to me, but no one had told me the truth either. And the cruellest part was that they didn't need to. I hadn't asked. I had never learnt to ask.

I was taught to listen, to obey, to make peace with whatever was handed to me. I was taught to smile when spoken to, to stay quiet when things didn't feel right, and to trust that someone older, someone wiser, someone male, would decide what was best for me. And so I did.

When I heard Amit's name, I built a story. When he spoke kindly, I imagined meaning. When my parents stayed vague, I filled in the blanks. No one corrected me, and I never asked them to.

I had written 'Durga loves Amit' on my trousseau box, and everyone saw it. My father saw it. He saw my joy, and he chose silence. He thought my illusion was softer than the truth. He believed, perhaps, that if I thought I was happy, I would become so.

And now I understood.

I had not been betrayed by one person or one

family. I had been shaped by silence—carefully, gently, but completely. I had been moulded into someone who could be led to a wedding and not know the name of her groom, someone who had learnt to follow without ever realizing that there was a choice.

They gave me lessons in obedience, but never in voice. They dressed me in traditions, but never asked me what I wanted to wear. They gave me rituals and customs and expectations, and I wore them all like ornaments I was supposed to be grateful for.

And now, as the last of those ornaments slipped away, I was left with something rawer, something truer.

I wasn't angry anymore. I wasn't defeated either.

I was simply aware—for the first time—that I had been living someone else's script, reading someone else's lines, and that I had the right to stop.

I heard the sound of a car pulling up. They had come to take me back.

I stood—not with resolve, not with revenge, but with a quiet recognition of myself. I didn't know what I would say. I didn't know what I would do. But I knew one thing with absolute clarity.

I was not just a daughter.

I was not just a bride.

I was not a mistake.

I was Durga.

What came before—you may call it destiny.

But what comes next? That, I choose.

4

Kinship in Exile

'As we bid adieu to our graduating class, we feel nostalgic and proud at once,' Father Sebastian said, addressing a sea of eager faces. 'We have not just educated you—we have polished our diamonds. Remember, education isn't just the degree you hang on your wall. It shines through your behaviour, your understanding and how you respond to the world around you. You represent one of the finest schools in this country—make sure you make us proud.'

The hall erupted with applause as he stepped back from the podium. My heart was racing, like everyone else's. This was the moment. The one we'd waited for throughout the year. The announcement of the Best Boy.

At Loyota, it wasn't just a title. For over a hundred years, the student honoured as 'Best Boy' earned a recommendation and full scholarship consideration for Oxford University. While the final admission decision rested with the university, the endorsement from Father Sebastian carried immense weight. For any student, it was a dream worth fighting for.

As we returned after a brief recess for snacks, tension hung in the air like humidity before a storm.

'Relax, Vinni,' I said, nudging him with my elbow. 'If not you, then who? You've aced everything—academics, sports, debates. You're basically a trophy shelf in human form.'

Vinayak smiled faintly. 'I've worked for it, Mazhar. No doubt. But Ranveer's been nothing short of stellar too. Something tells me today's his day.'

'Don't make me choose between my best friends,' I said. 'That's like choosing between biryani and butter chicken.'

He laughed. 'You and your food analogies.'

'Don't forget,' I said, 'there are three awards tonight. Imagine—Vinayak, Ranveer and Mazhar—the trio that left a mark on this batch.'

'Amen to that,' said Ranveer, joining us.

'Look at Fatso dreaming,' Vinayak teased. 'You didn't even show up for the prefect elections and expected to win. You were too busy hogging food or napping in the library.'

'Hey, I was living the good life—*la dolce far niente*,' I declared.

'La what now?' Vinayak asked, raising an eyebrow.

'The sweetness of doing nothing,' I said, grinning.

Just then, Father returned to the stage. 'Back to your seats, boys,' he called. 'Time for the moment you've all been waiting for.'

We slid into our chairs, hearts thumping.

'The Best Boy Award of the 2012 Session,' Father began, then paused deliberately—'goes to...Vinayak Agarwal!'

Vinni sprinted towards the stage, half in disbelief, half in fear that someone else might claim it in his place. That was so him—earnest, slightly panicked, deeply deserving.

Ranveer and I stood, clapping hard enough to sting our palms.

As the applause subsided, Father continued, 'As you all know, Vinayak will be endorsed for Oxford University, with full scholarship eligibility.'

The crowd roared. I swear I saw one teacher wiping away a tear.

Then came the next announcement.

'We also wish to honour the student who has balanced academic commitment with excellence in extracurriculars—especially in national-level sports and leadership. The boy who's made this school proud in interschool and interstate competitions...Ranveer Shetty.'

Ranveer whooped and shot out of his seat.

'Master Ranveer,' Father declared, 'will receive a full scholarship under the sports quota in any Indian university of his choice.'

Ranveer clutched his trophy like it were oxygen.

I pulled him into a hug as he returned. '*Mere do*

anmol ratan, my two precious gems' I whispered.

'This means my parents will finally believe in me,' Ranveer whispered. 'Especially my dad. He always said sports would take me nowhere.'

Vinni clapped him on the back. 'Flaunt your worth now. You've earned every bit of it.'

Then Father raised the mic again. 'Before we close, we have something special. As of this year, we've introduced a third honour—to recognize something just as important as academic or athletic brilliance: humanity. The award for "Outstanding Behaviour" goes to the student who has shown unwavering kindness, compassion and responsibility throughout his time here.'

My ears perked up. As he listed the acts—writing exams for an injured junior, fetching first aid, staying after school to tidy classrooms—I blinked. Those stories...they sounded familiar. Too familiar.

'So,' Father said, 'it is with great pride that I call on stage the first recipient of this award, Mazhar Khan.'

For a second, I didn't react. Ranveer elbowed me. 'It's you, Fatso. Go!'

I stood up slowly, disbelief spreading through me. I walked up to the stage, my legs feeling heavier than usual.

'Good deeds always find their way back to you,' Father said, handing me the award. 'Keep being you.'

'Mazhar,' he continued, 'will also receive a recommendation from me and a 50 per cent scholarship for further studies.'

I could barely speak. I looked at my friends—my brothers—and saw nothing but pride on their faces.

'You were right, Fatso,' Ranveer called. 'Vinayak, Ranveer and Mazhar—names carved into Loyota's legacy.'

‿

10 January 2022

Dear Mazhar,

Can you believe it's already been ten years since you graduated from Loyota High School? Time has flown.

We're organizing the 20th Loyota reunion in Dehradun on the weekend of 15-17 June. It would mean a lot to have you join us, along with your classmates. We'll send further details soon. For now, mark your calendar.

We hope to see you and relive those golden days.

Warm regards,

Father A. Sebastian
Principal, Loyota School

I didn't even stop to think. I replied with a prompt 'Yes.'

The email felt like a ray of sunlight after a long storm. Life had moved at breakneck speed. Between my career, responsibilities and life's chaos, I hadn't kept in touch with anyone. No Vinni. No Ranveer. No batchmates. Just scattered memories and dusty photographs in unopened drawers.

But now… Now I had a chance to go back. Not to the past—but to the people who had shaped it.

෴

15 June 2022

As I stepped through the familiar gates of Loyota School, I felt the years melting away.

The cool wind whipped through the southern corner of the campus—that same nostalgic breeze that once carried the scent of chalk dust, cheap cologne and anticipation. The walls looked the same, even after all these years. Faded in colour, but not in spirit.

My feet moved instinctively toward the corridor—our corridor. I could almost see myself—younger, louder, fatter—sitting cross-legged with a packet of chips and animatedly arguing whether Chelsea or Manchester United was the better team.

The sound of my shoes echoed with memories.

I headed towards the principal's office. Through the glass, I spotted an older man—frailer than I remembered but radiating the same energy.

'Welcome, my boy,' said Father Sebastian, standing up to greet me. His voice still had that unmistakable warmth, the kind that could both discipline and comfort.

Overwhelmed, I hugged him. It wasn't formality—it was instinct. He was more than a teacher. He had seen me grow, fall, laugh, cry…and somehow still remembered.

'I'm glad you came early,' he said. 'Most of your batchmates are flying in later today and will join us directly in the evening. We've arranged rooms in the hostel. You'll find yours waiting. But if you're free, come back early for tea. I'd love to catch up with my diamonds.'

As I turned to leave, a sudden question tugged at my heart. I stopped and glanced back.

'They're coming,' Father said, reading my thoughts before I could even speak. 'Vinayak and Ranveer. Should be here by afternoon.'

His ability to read us hadn't dulled with time.

The walk to the hostel was shorter than I remembered. Or maybe my legs had grown longer since those schoolboy days. I unlocked the old door to my former room and smiled.

There it was—my bunk bed. Nothing luxurious. No plush mattress. But that bed had held the most peaceful, unburdened sleep of my life. The kind of sleep that only comes when your biggest worry is an unfinished homework or a missed cricket catch.

I sank into it and felt a kind of quiet I hadn't felt in years. No ringing phones, no looming emails, no deadlines. Just wood creaking beneath memory. I drifted into sleep without even realizing it.

Later that evening, I stood before the mirror adjusting my red bowtie. For the first time, I really saw myself.

Gone was the chubby boy with a half-tucked shirt and perpetual runny nose. The mirror now reflected a man—polished, composed, moustached, even. But under the surface, I still felt like the same Mazhar. The

Fatso. The Dreamer. The Foodie. The Loyal Friend.

I stepped out, walking past the football ground, and just as I neared the mess, a familiar scent stopped me in my tracks. Freshly brewed ginger tea. And then... something else.

'Old Spice.' I turned.

'Always,' came the reply.

Ranveer stood there—taller, broader, sharper—but unmistakably Ranveer. My best friend. My childhood partner-in-crime. My teammate in every sense of the word.

We hugged. No words were needed.

◦

The school grounds looked majestic under the golden hue of dusk. Fairy lights twinkled like constellations across the open lawn. Round tables draped in white linen dotted the space. Waiters in black waistcoats carried trays of hors d'oeuvres. The Loyota Reunion had officially begun.

The laughter was real—but it carried a tone of restraint.

Old friends met as if they were strangers exchanging polite pleasantries. Gone were the slaps on the back, the bear hugs, the silly nicknames. Now it was handshakes and formal smiles.

Mazhar Khan. Someone actually called me that. Not Fatso. Not Khan Saab. Just...Mazhar Khan.

Ranveer noticed too. 'Feels weird, right?' he said,

sipping his ginger tea. 'Everyone's walking around like LinkedIn profiles at a networking brunch.'

I laughed, but it came out more like a sigh. 'Where are the boys who used to stick chewing gum on each other's backs and dunk heads in toilet bowls?'

'Apparently replaced by Regional Managers and Founders and Consultants,' he said, smirking.

It wasn't bitterness. It was grief. Not for the people—they were still here—but for the lost ease, the shared mischief, the uninhibited joy.

I scanned the crowd. 'Have you seen Vinni?'

A voice called out from behind: 'Hey Fatso! I'm here.'

We turned. There he was. Vinayak Agarwal. Our Vinni. Clad in a well-fitted suit, glasses perched on his nose, a little heavier around the eyes but unmistakably him.

We didn't say anything. We ran into each other's arms like children. No hesitation.

I pulled back first. 'You're late.'

'You're thinner,' Vinni replied, eyeing my bowtie. 'You look like a maître d' in a Parisian café.'

Ranveer chuckled. 'He's just upgraded from school canteen to Michelin star.'

Vinni laughed too, but then paused. 'I can't believe it's been eight years.'

We grabbed cups of tea and the packet of—what else—Uncle Chipps. Found our old corner near the corridor wall and sat down, just like we used to. A quiet spot, away from the buzz.

For a while, no one spoke.

Finally, I opened the packet and said, 'You know, Uncle Chipps is hard to find these days.'

Ranveer grinned. 'Bole mere lips, I love Uncle Chipps!'

We burst into laughter.

Vinni's voice dipped into something heavier. 'So… why didn't you two call me all these years?'

Ranveer sat up straighter. 'Why didn't you call us?'

'You guys were in India, I was far away—'

'Oh, please,' Ranveer cut in. 'As if distance has anything to do with a WhatsApp message.'

I stayed quiet for a second, then said, 'We all messed up. Life got fast. And maybe… Maybe we got scared of finding things changed.'

Ranveer's voice cracked a little. 'I sent both of you my wedding invite. Kept waiting. No replies. I tried calling. Once. Twice. Then I stopped.'

We all looked down.

The silence wasn't awkward. It was full—of guilt, of missed chances, of love.

Tears threatened to betray us, but Vinni broke the mood with a chuckle. 'This is turning into a Karan Johar film.'

I elbowed him. 'You should've seen me cry when I ran out of Maggi at midnight last week.'

We laughed again, gentler this time.

It wasn't perfect. The damage of years doesn't vanish in a night. But a crack had formed in the walls we'd built. And through it, warmth was flowing.

Vinni cleared his throat like someone bracing for an announcement. 'So... Do I go first?'

'Of course you do,' I said. 'You're the guy from Wall Street now.'

'Close,' he said with a smirk. 'New York City. I'm Sub-Head of Finance at American Express.'

Ranveer gave a low whistle. 'No way! That's massive, bro. I mean... Amex? Sub-head?'

'It's not a joke,' I said. 'He always aimed high and he got there.'

Vinayak nodded, but his eyes were soft. 'It's all true. New York's everything people say it is—loud, fast, relentless. You run just to stand still. The money's great, but so is the burnout.'

'And personal life?' I nudged.

'Ah. Now we get to the spice.' He smiled. 'I'm in a live-in relationship.'

Ranveer choked on his tea.

'You? Mr Traditions-and-Sanskars?'

'I know, right?' Vinni laughed. 'Life changes you. She's amazing—career-driven, grounded, independent. We both love each other but we're not ready for marriage just yet.'

'And your family is okay with it?' I asked gently.

'Reluctantly. At first they freaked out. But now... they've seen we're stable. We're happy. We pay rent together, cook together, binge-watch documentaries on weekends. It works.'

'You sound...grown up,' Ranveer said, half-teasing, half-impressed.

Vinni smiled wistfully. 'Cohabitation isn't some rebellion. It's a choice—for emotional honesty and practical sanity.'

We were quiet. Not out of judgement—but because we were processing how far we'd all come from school uniforms and curfews.

Then I turned to Ranveer. 'Alright, Mr Heartthrob. Your turn. Still surrounded by fangirls?'

He chuckled. 'Sort of. I'm a celebrity fitness trainer now. Own seven gyms in the city. Work with a few Bollywood stars. Life's good.'

'Wow,' Vinni said. 'Didn't I always say you'd end up famous?'

I leaned forward. 'But what about your love life? I'm bracing for some dramatic whirlwind romance here.'

Ranveer laughed, then paused. 'Actually... I had an arranged marriage.'

'What? You?' Vinni and I said in unison.

'I know it's hard to believe. But my parents insisted. And you know what? I went with it. Met Rishika through our families. We dated a bit. No fireworks at first, but she grew on me. She's thoughtful, fierce, kind. She makes my house a home.'

'That's so not the image I had in mind,' I said honestly.

He shrugged. 'Arranged doesn't mean loveless anymore. We met, we talked, we chose each other. Now it's about shared goals, support, kindness. Love comes in later, sometimes.'

'Like a slow-cooked biryani,' I offered.

'Exactly,' he smiled. 'And she's my biggest cheerleader.'

Vinayak nodded appreciatively. 'In New York, people look down on arranged setups. But yours...sounds real. And strong.'

'Thanks,' Ranveer said. 'Now, Fatso, your turn. Tell us how the kid who used to steal samosas from the canteen became India's Gordon Ramsay.'

I grinned. 'After Loyota, I joined the Institute of Hospitality Management. At first, it was just about eating well. But there, I discovered the joy of cooking.'

'Full circle,' Vinni muttered.

'That recommendation letter from Father Sebastian? It helped me get into the country's top culinary school. Then internships, long hours, a lot of burns and tears. Now, I'm Executive Chef at the Taj and I host cooking workshops worldwide.'

'Wow,' Vinayak whispered.

'And...I'm married. Court marriage. Small and simple. Just family.'

'Wait, what?' Ranveer blinked. 'You're married? Since when? And you didn't tell us?'

I looked down. 'I wanted to. I did. But it was all so low-key. I didn't think you'd fly in for a court signing.'

Vinni stared at me. 'You thought that little of us?'

'Not little. I was scared I had become...unimportant to you.'

There it was. The truth.

Ranveer exhaled, long and slow. 'We weren't strangers, Mazhar. We were just...lost.'

Silence again. But this time, we let it stretch.

Then Vinni brightened. 'Do you have kids?'

I smiled. 'A boy. Two years old. His name's Sai.'

'That's beautiful,' Ranveer said.

'It works for both families. My in-laws are South Indian Hindus and we're Muslim. Sai bridges that.'

'And how's fatherhood?' Vinni asked, leaning in.

'Tough,' I said. 'Rewarding. Confusing. We both work full-time, so we share responsibilities. I cook, bathe him, feed him, do homework. So does Aishwarya.'

Ranveer blinked. 'That's rare. And inspiring.'

'Some people call it "helping". But I'm not helping— I'm parenting. And I wish more dads saw it that way.'

Vinni put his hand on my shoulder. 'You're raising a kid and a mindset. That's real change.'

We looked at each other. All three of us.

A live-in partner. An arranged wife. A hands-on husband and father. Three different paths. Three different philosophies.

And still—the same boys who once jumped school walls for extra samosas.

Our tea cups were empty. The packet of Uncle Chipps, now just a foil memory, rustled in the breeze. But the stories we shared had filled something else— something that had been hollow for years.

Not just updates. Understanding.

Vinni leaned back against the wall and looked up at the darkening sky. 'You know,' he said, 'I've sat in dozens of boardrooms, but nothing feels as real as this corner.'

Ranveer smiled. 'Same. I've trained actors, won awards, but...this? This is the medal that was missing.'

'And me,' I said quietly. 'I've cooked for ambassadors, celebrities...but nothing compares to serving memories with you both tonight.'

Silence again. But now, it was rich. Full of warmth and forgiveness.

Then Vinni asked, softly, 'Why didn't we fight harder to stay in touch?'

Ranveer replied first. 'Because growing up tricks you. It tells you friendship is flexible. That it can stretch to any distance, any silence. But it's not elastic. It bruises.'

'And yet,' I added, 'we found our way back. Maybe that's what makes it stronger.'

A loud screech echoed across the ground—the microphone. Father Sebastian's voice, still commanding yet comforting, rang out.

'My dear boys,' he said, standing beneath the spotlight. 'Twenty-five years ago, you came to this institution as clay. You left as diamonds. And tonight, you return...as stars.'

Applause rippled through the crowd.

'Each of you,' he continued, 'has taken a different path. But remember, success isn't measured by your titles or your bank accounts. It's in your ability to stay human. To forgive. To remember. To love.'

We stood still, listening. A hush had fallen.

'And for those who wondered what they'd find here tonight—let it be this: You're never too far from who you used to be. And it's never too late to return.'

Ranveer held out his hand. I took it. Vinayak joined.

We walked—slowly, deliberately—towards the gathering. Not just to join the function. But to step, as brothers, into the light.

Around us, cheers rang out. Familiar voices called names. But we heard only one thing: Our own laughter. Our own bond. Intact. Tested. Timeless.

As Father raised a toast to 'Loyota Boys, Forever,' we raised our glasses in silent agreement.

We had come looking for the past. Instead, we found ourselves.

I smiled, eyes a little wet, and said, 'All these years... it was still there, wasn't it? Just a kinship in exile, waiting to find its way back.'

5

....

A Tuesday

Devesh had worn many titles in life—news anchor, editor-in-chief, columnist. In his quiet, Tier-III hometown, each milestone felt effortless, wrapped in the comfort of familiarity. But even frogs outgrow their wells and, eventually, the City of Dreams called him.

Mumbai wasn't as unforgiving as he'd feared—but it wasn't gentle either. The city tested one in invisible ways. It made one stand in long queues, chase late rent, stretch a freelance cheque, and yet somehow still whisper poetry through the window of a moving local train.

He had taken time—struggled with bylines, smiled through rejection emails, networked at awkward brunches—and slowly built a name. Not a big one, but one that was now called upon when an article needed heart.

He had thought he understood Mumbai. It was a beautiful contradiction—vada pav and masala dosa in the same breath as gourmet fusion food, slums nestled beneath the shadows of sky-high towers, Kolhapuri chappals tapping in rhythm with Armani shoes. The city didn't judge. It absorbed.

But cities are like mirrors—what you see depends on how you look.

One rainy Tuesday afternoon, the assignment came in like a casual text—one of those briefs tossed off with the ease of someone who didn't think twice. 'Simplicity', it read. That was the theme for this month's article.

Devesh almost scoffed aloud. Simplicity? He was the poster boy for it. A small-town man who still preferred All Out over fancy diffusers, who bought pens in bulk during stationery sales, who wore hand-me-down sweaters like heirlooms. What could possibly be simpler than the life he had left behind?

But that evening, when he sat at his desk to begin writing, his fingers hovered over the keyboard…and stayed there. Words didn't come. Instead, questions did.

Was simplicity just absence? Of clutter? Of ambition? Of makeup and marketing? Or was it something else— something harder to define?

He wrote three drafts. Then deleted them all.

On the fourth attempt, he found himself staring not at the screen, but at the small clay diya on his windowsill—a leftover from Diwali last year. He hadn't lit it in months. Dust clung to its edges. It looked simple. But it held layers—of tradition, nostalgia, a mother's call reminding him to light it each year.

That was when he realized the topic wasn't a shortcut. It was a maze. A puzzle wearing a plain face.

To clear his thoughts, he wandered to the beach. The breeze carried a comfort he hadn't felt since leaving home. Sitting on a bench near the shore, he let the waves settle his thoughts. When hunger tapped at his focus, he followed the scent of spice until he stood at a familiar crossroad—two signs for pav bhaji. One led into a glossy café. The other to a roadside stall lit by flickering bulbs.

The choice was reflexive. Authenticity, he believed, was second nature to people like him.

The food arrived hot and chaotic—red, buttery, vivid. He was just starting to lose himself in its taste when a luxury car honked nearby. From it stepped a woman—tall, poised, dressed in a bright red one-shoulder top and denim mini-skirt, heels clicking against the uneven ground. Her lipstick matched her blouse. Her presence cut through the haze like a siren.

He had noticed her before. Not often. Not clearly. But once or twice—crossing the street near the publishing office, phone in hand, dressed like someone who knew how to make an entrance. She had that walk, that aura—one that made heads turn but left no room for questions.

Instinctively, his guard went up.

These are the kind who taste street food for Instagram stories, he thought, *who bring their own cutlery to add irony.*

But even as the thought formed, he felt it scratch

against something inside him. Was he judging her—or protecting something in himself? A truth? A memory? A version of simplicity he didn't want to complicate?

And then—she smiled. Not at him. At two children running towards her. She knelt down, hugged them close, ruffled their hair like she'd done it every week. She waved at the stall owner and exchanged a few words. Then, she crossed the road and disappeared inside the café.

He turned, dazed, to the stall owner. 'Who is she?' he asked.

The man smiled. 'Madam owns the café. Some time ago, my kids went in asking for work. She told them they were too young. Said they belonged in school. I told her I couldn't afford to send them. So she helped me open this stall. Paid the licence fee, even helped with the setup. All she asked was that I promise to send them to school. Every Tuesday, she makes pasta for them—they'd once seen it on TV and asked her what it tasted like.'

He sat in stunned silence. The woman he had silently mocked—the magazine cover in red—had just rewritten every assumption he thought he understood.

Late at night, as he sat at his desk, the city lights blinking against the windowpane like distant fireflies, something inside him shifted.

He thought of the woman's pasta Tuesdays. Of the vendor's children and their wide-eyed wonder at a dish they'd only ever seen on television. And he thought of a boy—skinny, awkward, maybe thirteen—sitting on the floor of a tiny home in his hometown, eating with his fingers while watching a cookery show with his sister, pretending he, too, could one day afford what was on the screen.

That boy had once asked his mother why they didn't have a microwave.

'Because some things don't need speeding up,' she had said with a tired smile, turning rotis on the open flame.

Back then, he hadn't understood. He had felt embarrassed, almost ashamed, when city cousins visited and commented on the 'old-school' ways of his family. He had laughed along, just to belong.

And now here he was—older, supposedly wiser, still judging people by how far they stood from his own insecurities.

The realization came not like a thunderclap, but a slow, steady wave. He had left behind the town, the stove, the boy—but had brought the judgement with him. He had looked at the woman and seen not her actions but his discomfort.

I was not defending simplicity, he thought. *I was defending my version of it. One I had made too fragile to hold any contradiction.*

The article began to write itself, not as an argument but as a confession. A letting go. A reconciliation between the boy he had been and the man still trying to define himself by what he understood as 'authentic'.

Months later, he stood in front of a huge crowd, accepting an award for that very piece. That night, as he cradled the plaque they'd handed him, he thought of people whose names never made it into awards.

And he remembered Munish.

Devesh met Munish during his early days in Mumbai when he'd been assigned a profile piece on the elusive, internationally celebrated fashion photographer. He remembered being nervous, fumbling through his questions while Munish remained aloof, giving clipped answers.

Towards the end of the interview, he had blurted out, 'I'm from Jaspur too. Sector 6. Small world, right?'

Munish had only nodded. No warmth, no light in the eyes. Just a polite shrug before looking past him. It had confused him then. Offended him, even.

Why would someone turn cold at the mention of home?

He would later learn why.

In Jaspur, photography was for weddings and passports. Not a calling. Not a future. Munish's father ran a grocery store and believed a man's pride lived in numbers, not negatives. The boy who walked around clicking photos of sleepy lanes and old women sitting under the gallow tree had been dismissed as eccentric. Even dangerous. A dreamer with no grounding.

'What will photography give you?'

'Is this a career or a phase?'

'Mad boy... Always peering through that thing like he's too good for the world.'

But Munish saw things differently. His camera didn't record images—it revealed truths. The way some people looked away too fast. The way joy and sadness sometimes shared a frame.

Now his work appeared in glossy magazines. His art adorned gallery walls in cities that had never even heard of Jaspur. And ironically, the very people who once dismissed him now invited him for events.

'Please visit your school.'

'Come inspire the students.'

'Your story can change lives.'

But he never returned.

Not out of bitterness or anger. But because some mirrors, once shattered, need not be pieced together. Some silences are louder than applause.

In remembering Munish, Devesh felt something settle in him—like the last piece of a long-unfinished puzzle. The woman in red. The vendor's children. Munish's lens. All stories of quiet defiance. All carriers of a truth far more powerful than appearance.

Sometimes, the limited knowledge people hold becomes the very lens through which they judge others. They see the world not as it is—but only as far as they themselves have walked.

And then, there are people like Munish—those who see further, walk alone and wait for the world to catch up.

In this realization, Devesh found clarity.

Whether it was the woman who fed street children or the man who saw beauty in shadows, the truth wasn't in perception. It was in constancy. It lay in knowing who you are. In standing your ground. In being kind, creative and brave—even when misunderstood.

Mumbai had always been described as a monster or

a miracle. But to him, it had become something quieter. A mirror.

It didn't teach. It reflected.

In its cluttered streets and café windows, he had seen his own assumptions—laid bare. In pasta bowls and red lipstick, in school shoes and camera shutters, he had witnessed kindness, resilience, grace. Not in grandeur, but in contradiction.

Devesh had come to the city thinking he would write about it. Chronicle it. Explain it. But Mumbai wasn't a place you explained. It was a place that explained you.

That night, he didn't feel triumphant. He felt clean, honest.

Like someone who had stopped trying to edit the world—and had finally started reading it properly.

6

....

Backup Plan

A cluster of men dressed in full red attire pounced on me the moment I stepped off the train, nearly choking my breath. No, it wasn't a terrorist attack. Just a common sight at Indian railway stations—the infamous rush of coolies. They compete like warriors, each trying to be the first to snatch your luggage. Whoever grabs your bag first claims you as their rightful customer. I hadn't experienced this sort of chaos in years.

I struggled to cut through the crowd, my feet barely touching the ground. I wasn't walking—just drifting, carried by the push from the sea of people behind me. Shoulders brushed mine, elbows jabbed and the stench of sweat was overwhelming. I nearly fainted. Travelling in aeroplanes had pampered me.

Yet, surprisingly, the station was cleaner than I had

expected. Gone were the days of overflowing trash and relentless hawkers. Now, small government-run stalls had replaced the chaos of street vendors. *Progress*, I thought. Developing India indeed.

I suddenly became nostalgic. Memories surged and I was transported to my childhood. Every summer, we'd travel from Ranchi to Delhi to visit my mother's side of the family. It was a ritual. The long train journey filled us with excitement. Maa would pack all kinds of food and Papa always carried board games to keep us entertained. The station, for us, was a treasure trove. We never boarded the train without buying comics from the hawkers—I had an impressive *Chacha Chaudhary* collection. I used to fancy myself thinking faster than a computer, like him.

My sister Anjali and I would roam the train compartments looking for kids our age, striking up instant friendships, playing Ludo or antakshari, giggling with strangers. The non-AC three-tier coach in the sweltering summer was far from comfortable, but we didn't care. Maa would wet towels and hang them on the window bars to cool the hot breeze that filtered in. We carried soaps to wash our hands and checked our luggage locks a dozen times before sleeping. Those were the days. Unfiltered, magical, raw.

I was pulled back into the present as I reached the auto stand. I showed the driver an address and climbed in. The road leading to the city was lined with flowers and trees, unusually calm and peaceful—no loud honks or crowds. 'Peace,' I whispered as we entered the steel city of India, Jamshedpur.

We passed buildings named after gemstones—Emerald, Topaz, Ruby—until we stopped outside Sapphire. As I turned to pay the fare, I heard my name being shouted from a balcony. There stood Rati. Her voice was as familiar as home. She waved from the fourth floor, beckoning me to come up.

There were three flats on the floor, but Rati's was unmistakable. Her name, carved in gold on a piece of mural art, adorned the door. A small board below read 'Sanskrit Class'. Before I could knock, she opened the door. We hugged tight, tears soaking our cheeks. Years had passed, but the bond hadn't faded a bit.

Her daughter stepped forward and touched my feet, a gesture so tender it made my heart clench. I wondered what I'd been doing wasting away in Europe all these years.

'Two cups of ginger tea?' Rati called out to her daughter.

'You remember?' I asked, my voice cracking.

'Of course,' she smiled.

We grew up in Ranchi together. From school to college, we were childhood friends—diaper buddies. Rati always called me her best friend, though I held Anjali a little closer. My younger sister was my soulmate. We did everything together—from playing carrom in our galli to sneaking out to eat the famous chilli paneer from Kaveri. Rati never resented our closeness. She appreciated it. She was always the second closest person in my life and she embraced that with grace.

Her home was simple, bright, warm. A 3 BHK with

minimal furniture, a few framed photos, an oversized wall clock and a Laughing Buddha. A yellow-accent wall lit up the room like sunshine. Her balcony—her favourite spot—was decked with flowerpots and creepers, and a three-seater swing swayed gently in the breeze. There was something very peaceful about her home. No frills, just warmth.

As we munched on thekua and sipped our tea, Rati told her daughter about how I had convinced her to give Raghav a chance in college. He had chased her for months and she kept rejecting him—he wasn't from Ranchi, and she couldn't imagine leaving her family. But I had told her, 'Home is where the heart is. A man who loves you deeply is worth adjusting for.' She still credits me for her happy marriage.

I didn't speak of my own. Didn't want to ruin the moment. I hid my pain under a polite smile.

After tea, I feigned exhaustion and took a long nap—not from fatigue, but to delay the purpose of my visit. By the time I woke up, it was night. Raghav had returned from work. Rati ushered me to the dinner table.

Before I could apologize for sleeping so long, she jumped in, 'Train journeys are exhausting. You're used to Europe's chill and now this heat! Glad you caught some sleep.'

She always knew how to ease my discomfort.

Raghav welcomed me warmly. 'You haven't changed. Europe's done good—you look ravishing!'

I smiled sheepishly. It had been a long time since I'd shared a meal with someone—anyone. I wasn't unmarried, widowed or orphaned. I had a family in Europe: a husband and a son. But that meal was the first time in years I felt...human again.

Between Anjali and me, I was always Baba's favourite—the apple of his eyes. Ours was a simple middle-class family, the kind where mangoes in May and wins in galli cricket were reasons enough to celebrate. But happiness and sorrow, they walk hand in hand, don't they? And neither ever stays forever.

Just when I was finishing college, Baba was diagnosed with terminal cancer. He didn't have much time left, but he wanted to see both his daughters settled. So, without too many choices, we were married off—I to a businessman in Europe, Anjali to a businessman in Ranchi. There were whispers, of course. Some said Baba had favoured me, marrying me off to an NRI. That I was lucky, chosen.

Baba passed away right after our weddings. Amma followed soon after, consumed by grief. Losing your parents feels like your backbone breaking—you're still standing, but everything feels wrong.

At least I had Anjali. She was my anchor. We promised to never let go of each other, to always be each other's home.

In the beginning, Europe was a dream. The snow, the beauty, the quiet—it all felt magical. I was treated like a queen. My husband seemed caring, generous. It was a honeymoon phase that felt like it would never end. But then, slowly, reality unfolded.

When I gave birth to our son, I expected joy. But he

seemed...disappointed. Said it was too soon. The warmth faded. I began to see the cracks. What I thought was love was novelty—he had simply been discovering his 'new toy,' as he once said jokingly, not realizing how deeply it hurt.

With time, I was reduced to a showpiece. I'd dress up, wear makeup, speak in polished English to impress his clients. Some of them crossed lines and he never objected. I wasn't a wife—I was an accessory or may be someone necessary, to run a household and make a family in a faraway land.

He wasn't violent. But he brought other women home. And I couldn't object. I was trapped in silence, watching my dignity bleed out slowly, one compromise at a time. I stayed. For my son. Only for him. I wanted him to grow up in a complete family, not torn between bitter parents.

My husband controlled every penny—I only received a 'household allowance'. Enough to buy groceries. I kept saving for my escape plan, bit by bit, from the cash gifts my family gave.

Rati had noticed my silence. That night, as we cleared the table and tucked Risha into bed, she brought out two cups of her ginger lemon tea. We settled into her swing on the moonlit balcony. The breeze wrapped around us like a quiet lullaby.

'You've been quiet,' she said, gently holding my hand.

'I'm just tired,' I replied.

'No, Richa. I've known you all my life. What's wrong?'

I broke down. Tears poured before words did. Rati held me while I shook. 'There's no problem too big, Richa,' she whispered. 'Speak.'

I told her everything. My failing marriage. My silent suffering. How I endured it all for the sake of my son, saving every penny I could for the day I'd leave.

When my son turned eighteen, I felt I could finally reclaim my voice. I met a lawyer discreetly, filed the initial papers, gathered what documents I could. It wasn't much, but enough to begin. My plan was simple: speak to my son, return to India and rebuild our lives. Fortunately, I had ₹30 lakh tucked away in India.

But life doesn't follow our scripts.

One evening, he sat me down and said he was in love—with a classmate—and moving in with her. My legs gave way. My dreams cracked open. When I told him about the divorce, my years of silence, my sacrifices—he didn't flinch.

My son had always admired his father. The way he dressed, the way he commanded a room, his clipped tone and easy confidence—it all left a mark. Even as a child, he would mimic his father's mannerisms, roll his eyes at my hesitations, correct my English. He loved me, I never doubted that, but somewhere along the way, love became layered with quiet condescension.

I remember one dinner party vividly. I had a headache and my husband was entertaining a few clients at home. I whispered to my son, 'Can you ask Papa if we can wrap up early tonight? I'm not feeling well.'

He gave me a blank look. 'It's just one evening,

Mum. Don't spoil the mood,' he said and walked away.

Small things like that. Easy to overlook.

'Why now?' he asked, brows drawn. 'All these years, you acted like everything was normal. I never saw you unhappy. Why change everything now?'

'I waited for you to grow up,' I whispered, 'so I could spare you the pain. I did this all for you.'

He stood, arms folded. 'You can't protect someone by hiding the truth. I've built a life here. A relationship.' He paused, then added, 'You should've told me earlier. You can't expect me to drop everything and start over in a country I barely know. You're being selfish.'

His words sliced through the illusion I had nurtured all these years. The son I had protected had become a stranger. I tried once more to reason, but he had made up his mind. He left. No goodbye. Just a closed door and fading footsteps.

I flew to Ranchi. Anjali knew my dream—to come back, start fresh, live with self-respect.

She welcomed me, though clearly surprised. 'I'm glad you're here, Didi,' she had said. 'We'll figure something out.'

But something about her smile felt off. I had barely settled into Anjali's guest room when the unease began to flicker—small things. Her hesitations. The way she didn't meet my eyes.

That night, I lay awake, thinking about the ₹30 lakh I had entrusted to her years ago. It had always been my emergency parachute. I reminded myself that Anjali was family. She would never—

But the thought didn't leave me.

Few days passed, and as I regained my emotional strength, I decided to talk about my divorce and my plan to settle in Ranchi to Anjali. One fine afternoon, when her kids were at school and my brother-in-law was at work, we sat down to chit-chat, just the two of us. I cautiously told Anjali about everything—from applying for divorce to leaving Europe permanently.

Anjali listened, lips sealed, eyes unreadable. After a long silence, she finally spoke, 'This is…a lot… I mean, leaving everything? After so long? How can you take such a big decision all of a sudden? You spent so many years of your life with that man…why leave him now?'

'Nothing is sudden,' I said, trying to remain calm. 'You know everything I've been through. You've read every letter, heard every sob. I was holding on only for my son. Now he's grown and has his own life and I want to live the rest of my life with dignity.'

She still looked dazed. 'But this is India, Didi. Here, a divorced woman doesn't have it easy. People talk, judge. Think about Maa and Baba. How would they feel?'

'They'd feel proud that I chose self-respect over submission,' I snapped. Her concern felt like a betrayal.

'I just… I don't want you to struggle, Didi,' she murmured, eyes dodging mine. 'And even if you want to start afresh, how will you survive here alone?'

'I have the money,' I replied, my voice shaking now. 'The thirty lakhs I kept with you all these years. I'll use that to begin.'

Her face drained of colour. She looked away.

'I... I was meaning to talk to you about that.'

I felt the room tilt slightly. 'Talk to me about what?'

'I... I don't have it,' she whispered.

'What do you mean?'

She hesitated. 'During notebandi, everything went upside-down. Our business crumbled. Moneylenders hounded us. The police came. My husband almost got arrested. I panicked. I used your money to save our home.'

My ears rang.

'You what?'

'I didn't think. I had to protect my family.'

'And me?' I asked, my voice barely a breath. 'Didn't you think about me even once?'

'I did. But it was chaos, Didi. I had no choice.'

I sat still. Numb. Not angry. Not sad. Just hollow.

'I know I should've told you,' she added quickly, 'but I always meant to return it. I just needed time.'

'Years of sacrifice. Trust. And you used my only security like pocket change,' I whispered.

'You think it was easy for me? I couldn't watch my husband go to jail while I had money in the house. Whether it was mine or yours, it didn't matter then.'

'I need to live,' I finally said. 'Give me the papers to the house. I'll sell my share. I'll start over.'

She stiffened. 'You have no share.'

'What?'

'We had the house transferred. We've lived there for ten years. Paid taxes, made repairs. The papers are in our name now. You have no claim.'

I stared at her. My childhood home, the one place I thought would anchor me, had been signed away.

'So now you're erasing my rights, too?'

'I have two daughters. I need money to get them married. You have a son. A husband. A family. You chose to leave. Why ruin everything to chase respect?'

I walked out of her house, not even crying. I had been betrayed—again.

I had one last hope: a childhood savings account in a local bank. Maybe a lakh, enough for a rented room, at least.

But when I reached the bank, it was shuttered. A notice flapped in the wind. 'Permanently closed. Bankrupt.'

My knees gave way. Everything I had counted on— gone. Just like that.

I boarded a train and came to Jamshedpur. No plan. Just instinct. Just the need to be held by someone who truly cared.

When I finished speaking, Rati didn't offer sympathy. She didn't say 'I'm sorry,' or call my sister names. She just held me. Gently. Quietly. It was enough.

Then she asked, 'What have you thought of next?'

'Nothing,' I whispered, hollow again.

'That's great,' she replied with a sparkle in her voice.

I blinked. 'What's great about it?'

She smiled. 'If you haven't planned anything yet, it means you're open to building something completely new. That's a gift, Richa. Blank pages are blessings.'

I didn't respond. My mind was too cluttered for optimism.

The next day dragged on. I didn't step outside my room. I lay curled on the mattress, thoughts spinning endlessly. Not once did Rati come in to prod or advise. She left me alone with my grief—and I resented it a little. Wasn't she supposed to console me? Hold my hand? Say the right things?

The following evening, she gently asked me to come sit in the drawing room. Her Sanskrit class was about to begin. One by one, children filed in. Rati greeted each by name, with a smile that reached her eyes. Her love for teaching radiated from every gesture. The students adored her. She recited verses, explained meanings, asked questions, clapped for correct answers. I watched in silence.

And for the first time in days, I felt something stir within me. A quiet kind of awe. The way Rati found joy in giving knowledge, in building others, was beautiful.

After the class ended, we hopped into her car to pick up Raghav from work. I wasn't in the mood to go anywhere, but she insisted. Outside his office, he climbed into the backseat, greeting us with a cheerful, 'The golden girls are here!'

We drove to a street-side food stall.

'Come on,' Raghav grinned. 'This is Jamshedpur's famous litti chokha. Not trying it is practically illegal.'

I smiled faintly and agreed.

He wasn't wrong. The piping hot litti—wheat balls baked to perfection and dunked in desi ghee—paired with spicy chokha made of mashed aubergine and green chillies, exploded with flavour. Each bite melted on my tongue and for a brief moment, I forgot to be sad.

Later, we strolled through Jubilee Park. Families picnicked, children ran through manicured paths, couples sat holding hands near the musical fountains. The park shimmered with soft light. We reached a rose garden and there, for the first time, I saw a purple rose.

Something about that bloom—the unexpected colour, the delicate defiance—touched me.

On the drive back, we sang along to old songs. I don't remember when I fell asleep that night. I just remember not hurting quite as much.

The next morning, I woke up early and joined Rati for her walk. She introduced me to her neighbours, the watchman, her chaiwala, her fellow walkers. Everyone greeted her warmly. There was respect in their voices, admiration. And again, I felt that stirring.

Back home, I offered to make coffee. European style.

'You don't have to—'

'I want to,' I insisted.

We carried the cups to her favourite spot—the balcony swing.

She took a sip and sighed. 'Delicious.'

Then she turned to me. 'What now?'

I sighed. 'I don't want to go back, but I don't have money. I came here relying on my savings. They're gone.'

She nodded. 'See, I know you were upset that I didn't console you. But I didn't want to make your pain a spectacle. I wanted you to feel it, sit with it and emerge strong. That's how healing happens.'

I looked down, ashamed for having misunderstood her silence.

'But you made one mistake, Richa,' she continued. 'You depended on the wrong thing.'

'What do you mean?'

'You put your faith in money, in people. You forgot the one thing no one can take from you—yourself.'

I frowned. 'I don't understand.'

She quoted, 'Education and talent are the two things that cannot be stolen by a thief, nor seized by a king, nor divided among heirs. They remain with you forever, even as you spend them.'

It was something our old Sanskrit teacher used to say. I had forgotten.

'You saved money, but money can vanish. Banks collapse. People betray. But talent? That's yours.'

'I have no talents,' I said quietly. 'Not like you. You're good at teaching. I... I was just a decorative doll in Europe.'

Rati frowned. 'Not true. You were a brilliant classical dancer, remember?'

I looked away. 'That was another life. I haven't danced in a decade.'

'Fine. Then what have you been doing all these years?'

I laughed bitterly. 'Wearing makeup. Dressing up. Smiling through business dinners. Entertaining clients. Speaking in refined English. Hosting like a trained doll. I stopped being a person and became a prop. I smiled when I had to, spoke when expected, sat through business dinners like I belonged—but it was all performance.'

'Exactly!' she clapped.

'What's to celebrate in that?' I asked, confused.

'This is a small town, Richa. Girls here are brilliant at academics, but they lack exposure. They need grooming. Confidence. Accent. Presence. You could teach that.'

'Me? Open grooming classes?'

'Why not? My daughter was just telling me how impressed she is by you. Let her be your first student.'

'I have no place, Rati. I can't start something from nothing.'

She reached across the table and held my hand. 'Use my living room. When you outgrow it, we'll find a bigger space. You can pay me rent once you're earning.'

Tears welled in my eyes. 'I can't take more favours from you.'

'This isn't charity. This is you, rising again. And I'm just here with the ladder.'

Just then, Risha walked in, rubbing her eyes. She hugged me and whispered, 'Your first student is ready.'

I laughed through my tears.

'Where's my advance fee?' I teased.

She giggled. 'One cup of ginger tea, coming up.'

I smiled. I was still standing. I didn't need anyone else to catch me.

I had always been my own backup plan.

7

The Purple Stone

While wandering through the bustling flea market of Arpora, I found myself drawn to a whirl of oddities—stalls run mostly by Russians, selling everything from handmade soaps to jars of creams with enchanting fragrances. One scent curled its way into my senses so thoroughly that I walked over, inhaled deeply and bought the jar without a second thought.

Further down, I spotted a quirky kiosk displaying bohemian jackets with ruffled sleeves and neon-tinted, artfully torn jeans. Bold, wild, too edgy for someone like me. I admired them from afar, unsure if I could ever carry off such unapologetic flair.

What struck me was how few Indian sellers there were. Maybe that's what made this corner of the beach feel so surreal, like a bubble tucked away from the rest of the world. I turned a corner and found myself drawn to a table crowded with coloured stones, tall incense sticks, tarot cards and neat bundles of sage. The display seemed to hum with energy.

'Hello, beautiful lady. I am Richard,' said a bald, fair-skinned Russian with a genial smile.

I examined the bowls of sage—each labelled differently. White sage from Australia; green sage from Ghana.

'What are these for?' I asked, curious.

'To clear negative energy,' Richard replied. 'Burn them in the evening. Leave your window open. You'll feel the negativity leave the house with the smoke.'

I raised an eyebrow. If that were true, why don't we just set fire to entire forests of sage and purify the whole world? The thought made me laugh under my breath.

Then, a bright, round, purple stone caught my eye. It gleamed outrageously under the bright moonlight, like something magical.

'What's this?' I asked, picking it up.

'It's beautiful, no?' he said. 'It represents truth and honesty. Wear it, keep it close, and those around you will be more honest. Even you will speak your truth more easily.'

I chuckled, slipping the stone's black thread over my head. 'I'm not sure if I need the honesty, but it definitely looks cool on me, Richard.'

After paying, I pulled out a cigarette and found a quiet spot with a sea view. I lit it and inhaled slowly, watching the endless waves crash—scary in their wildness, yet oddly soothing. Like a child, I knelt and traced my name in the sand with one finger. Yatree.

Why had my parents named me that? Ravi once remarked maybe they knew I'd live up to it. That I would become a wanderer.

I dialled his number again. Still off. I missed him. In that moment, I imagined curling into his arms in this beautiful place. As a warm gust of wind tangled my hair, a familiar scent floated in the air.

Am I missing him so much that I can smell him now?

My stomach growled, snapping me back to reality. It was already twilight. Holidays always do that—blur the edges of time. I wandered over to a shack nearby where a giant crab sat in a glass display, tempting enough to make my mouth water. But ordering crab alone felt too indulgent. That's the thing about certain foods—you need company to enjoy them fully.

Humans aren't built for aloneness, not really. We crave someone to talk to, to laugh with, to split food and secrets. I settled on a plate of fries and a glass of wine and perched myself near the counter, hoping they'd hurry with my order.

The music inside was upbeat. A familiar song—ours—started playing. Rihanna's 'We Found Love'. It made me smile, then sway slightly with the rhythm, the beat tugging at forgotten memories.

As the song faded out, a voice crackled through the speakers: 'This next one's dedicated by Ravi…to his love, Anna.'

I froze. The name hit me like a slap. No. It can't be.

My eyes darted around the shack. At a table near the bar, a familiar profile turned sideways. Tall, lean frame. That same absentminded way of adjusting his glasses. My heart dropped.

It was Ravi. Laughing. Clinking glasses. With a girl.

I stood still, trying to process the sight. Maybe I was mistaken. I blinked, looked again. No. It was him, unmistakably him—my Ravi, except he was smiling like a stranger. Like someone who had moved on.

Every step I took towards him felt heavier than the last. I wanted to scream, to vanish, to wake up. He finally looked up—his jaw slackening a bit when he saw me. But he didn't flinch. Didn't stand up. Didn't hide the girl.

She looked young. Pretty in a simple way. She glanced at me, unsure. I ignored her completely.

'Seriously, Ravi?' I whispered, the words catching in my throat.

He stood up slowly, saying nothing. Fury bubbled inside me—shame, disbelief, and confusion crashing in one nauseating wave.

I took a step closer. 'Who is she?' I demanded. 'Is this some kind of joke?'

Still, he said nothing. That calm, composed face—it unnerved me more than any apology could.

'Is it a fling? An affair? Are you too ashamed to admit you're cheating on me with—her?' My voice trembled with pain.

He didn't respond.

I reached for his wrist, desperate to yank him away, to force a conversation somewhere private. 'Come with me to the hotel,' I snapped. 'We're not talking about this in front of your...your distraction.'

I still believed, somewhere deep inside, that he couldn't possibly be serious. That she was just a momentary lapse, someone who'd latched on to him, not someone he truly wanted.

But he didn't move. Instead, he gently took my hand and led me to a nearby chair. I sat, legs giving way under the weight of disbelief. He knelt beside me, his eyes soft. The sea that once sounded like music now roared like grief.

He reached up to caress my head. I recoiled.

'You have to listen to me, Yati,' he said quietly. 'Please. Just listen.'

A chill ran through me, despite the heavy Goan heat. Something was very wrong.

'I need to be honest,' he began, his voice barely above a whisper. 'Not to justify myself. Just...to explain.'

I stared at him, my chest tightening with each word.

'You've been my best friend, Yati. That's how we started. That's how we grew. And for years, I was just in awe of you. Your spirit, your courage, your hunger to live fully. You never just existed—you expanded. Everywhere you went, you took up space with this fierce energy. And me... I admired it. I tried to catch up.'

He paused. I looked away, unsure if I wanted to hear the rest.

'I'm not like you. I've never been. Remember Disneyland? You were riding roller-coasters, laughing like a kid, and I was sitting on a bench, watching you from a distance. I wasn't bored—I was happy. Watching you glow made me feel joy. But part of me longed for someone who'd sit beside me on that bench. Someone quiet. Still. Like me.'

My throat felt dry. I didn't say a word.

'I know your wanderlust isn't a phase or a hobby—it's your identity. It's your career. You travel because it fuels you. But it exhausts me. Not your journeys. Just... the distance. The absence. You were always a phone call away, and yes, we talked, loved, shared...but I craved your presence. Not virtually. Physically. Emotionally. Fully.'

I felt my jaw clench. The ache in my chest deepened. 'So it's about sex?' I snapped. 'You needed someone to hold? To touch? Is that all?'

'No,' he said, shaking his head. 'It's not about sex. It's about nearness. About needing someone beside me at the end of the day. Someone who's not sending love through postcards or packages or poems...but someone who just sits across the table and asks how my day was.'

He was trembling slightly now, even if his voice stayed calm.

'Your gestures—your surprise gifts from faraway lands, your long letters quoting Gulzar and Ghalib—they were beautiful. But they made me feel smaller. I'd send you a short "I love you", and it felt like nothing next to your pages of poetry. You were grand. And I... I felt average.'

'You think I needed you to match me?' I whispered. 'That I wasn't content with your simple love?'

'I don't blame you,' he said gently. 'I blame myself—

for not saying it more clearly. I hinted at things, sure. I'd say I missed you, or that I didn't like long-distance. But I never really let you know how heavy it all felt. How much I was shrinking inside.'

The words pierced deeper than I expected.

'You were always the star in every room, Yati. You'd walk in and people noticed. And I loved that,' he continued. 'But I wanted to feel noticed too. I wanted to feel seen when I stood next to you… You were perfect… And I wanted someone imperfect. Someone who didn't shine so bright that I felt invisible.'

I stared at him, stunned. Wounded. His words echoed inside me like footsteps in an empty hall.

'So that's it?' I said. 'You found someone quieter. Simpler. Someone who doesn't make you feel small.'

He looked down, almost ashamed, but not quite.

'She's not a replacement,' he said softly. 'Her name is Anna. We met a few months ago, while you were away shooting your show in Europe. She's a schoolteacher. She reads bedtime stories to children and bakes her own bread. She doesn't quote poetry. She doesn't fly across continents. But when I'm with her, I feel…enough. She makes me feel seen. And steady.'

The ache rose up my throat like bile.

'So this average girl—this girl, who doesn't challenge you, doesn't intimidate you—that's who you love now?'

He hesitated. 'I don't know if love is the right word yet. But I feel peace… It wasn't serious at first—we were just talking, then seeing each other quietly. But somewhere in that stillness, I realized how much I longed for peace. With her, I don't feel like I'm always behind. I don't have to catch up with her.'

I burst into tears. Guttural and unrestrained, raw like an open wound. 'And what about me, Ravi? What about us? Everything we were—everything we shared—was that not love?'

'It was love,' he said, his voice gentle. 'It was deep and real. You brought colour and fire into every corner of my life. And maybe that's exactly why I couldn't hold on—I was never sure I belonged in that kind of brightness.'

His calm stung more than any rage would have. I wanted him to fight for me. To deny it. To say he was confused. But he didn't. He simply sat there, sorrowful and steady.

'I'm sorry for being honest,' he added.

That word—honest—it struck a strange chord. I straightened up, wiped my tears, and looked him dead in the eye.

'No, Ravi,' I said. 'You're not being honest. You're mistaking validation for love. Anna doesn't love you more. She just makes you feel less threatened. That's not honesty—it's comfort. There's a difference.'

He opened his mouth, but I didn't let him speak.

'I was never too much,' I continued. 'You just decided you weren't enough. That's your story, not mine. You think you've found peace, but really, you've just found someone who won't challenge your reflection.'

I stood up, my limbs shaking but my spine straight. 'You say I took the limelight. But maybe the real problem is you were afraid to stand in it with me.'

He looked away.

I turned, walked past Anna without a glance, and stepped back on to the sand. The sea shimmered under the moonlight, wild and alive.

I reached for the black thread around my neck. The purple stone pulsed against my skin. For a moment, I held it in my palm, feeling its smooth weight. Then I slipped it off and laid it gently on the sand beside me. Not to abandon it—but to let it rest. I didn't need a stone to name my truth anymore. I had walked right into it, barefoot and whole.

I wandered down the shore where some kids were building sandcastles in the dark. They laughed without care, sculpting fragile kingdoms in the moonlight.

Without thinking, I joined them—knees in the sand, hands moving freely.

Maybe that's what honesty really is. Not loud declarations or neat endings. Just choosing, again and again, to be who you are—even when it hurts.

8

....

Stumble, Fall, Rise

A man was hunched over his quantitative analysis paper, solving one question after another, the timer ticking beside him. Hours had passed. His limbs were numb from staying in the same posture and his fingers throbbed with fatigue. He needed tea—desperately.

He called out to Kaalu, his cousin and roommate, but there was no reply. Dragging his legs across the cold floor, he stretched the tingling back into his feet. Still no sign of Kaalu—neither in the bathroom nor tucked in any corner of their cramped room.

Disheartened and too drained to make tea himself, Aman reached for his last resort—his phone—and dialled Riya. She was his solace in this city away from home, his constant. Yes, she was his blessing in disguise; if it weren't for her, it would have been difficult to survive here in Jaipur.

They both were from Sikar and were now studying in the same college. Riya, pursuing her BEd, dreamt of becoming a teacher. Aman was preparing for CAT, aiming for a top business school to transform his father's legendary sweet shop into a modern venture.

Riya's phone, tucked beneath her pillow as always, buzzed. She wasn't in deep sleep—never when it came to Aman.

'Hi,' she answered softly.

Aman smiled. Her voice was his balm. Unlike most couples their age, their conversations revolved not around gossip or grand promises but around mock tests, weak topics and performance graphs.

They longed to hold hands, to eat pandit ki kulfi outside Hawa Mahal, to sit by the jheel feeding fish and whispering dreams. But they had chosen something greater—for now. Their careers came first. They reminded each other why they were here, in this city of distractions, holding on to a plan they'd made together. Aman's mock tests were just a week away. For now, love could wait.

Before hanging up, he whispered the line he always did, 'Keep shining, my Dhruv Tara.'

Riya smiled. She always did when he said that.

Moments after the call ended, Kaalu strolled in.

Before Aman could ask, Kaalu shot a question: 'Who were you talking to?'

Aman hesitated, then replied, 'Riya.'

'Oh, that masterniji,' Kaalu chuckled.

It baffled him how someone like Riya—intelligent, graceful and from a well-off family—would settle for a profession like teaching. In his view, she was throwing away her potential for a modest paycheck, when she could've easily chosen a more lucrative path. Though he dismissed her choices, deep down he admired her—she was out of his league, and he knew it.

When Aman asked where he'd been, Kaalu deflected, dodged, then offered to make tea. It was only after repeated prodding that he admitted he had been at Rajmandir Theatre watching the latest movie.

Aman was stunned. 'Your mock tests are next week,' he reminded him. 'This isn't the time to fool around.'

Kaalu shrugged. 'That's the difference between small-town boys like us and the metro kids here. We slog like labourers, chasing dreams, while they balance study with life. They take breaks, breathe and still succeed. That's their secret.'

His words lingered with Aman longer than he expected. Maybe, just maybe, Kaalu had a point. Maybe that's why others in the class were outperforming him. Still, Aman shook his head. 'I can't afford to waste time. Too much syllabus left.'

‿✎

The week passed in books and mock papers. When the tests were done and done well, Aman couldn't wait to meet Riya. He picked up the phone, heart racing.

She, meanwhile, was already ironing her favourite white chikankari kurta and blue denim—the outfit she reserved for special days.

Riya believed white never masked anything. It revealed the truth, reflected purity. And she was proud of her truth.

Aman called, brimming with excitement. 'The papers went great—I think I did well!'

Before he could ask her out, Riya cut in, 'Meet me outside Birla Temple this evening. I made a vow—if your exams went well, I'd offer peda to Krishna.'

She always had a way of surprising him with her small gestures, quiet but brimming with love. At that moment, Aman knew—he was lucky to have her.

Aman, ever the simple boy, reached for his usual outfit: a crisp, pale pink shirt and navy blue pants. He avoided T-shirts and jeans; he believed shirts gave a person gravity, made them look grounded and grown.

He remembered what his school law teacher had once said—'Clothes inspire conduct.' A doctor feels like a lifesaver in scrubs; a lawyer's black coat sharpens his argument. Attire wasn't just appearance—it was alignment with identity. That philosophy stayed with Aman. Though his formal style didn't match his age or setting, his tall frame carried it well.

As he sprayed deodorant under his arms, he hummed, 'Aaj main upar, aasman neeche, today I am above and the sky is below…'

Kaalu entered the room, having heard Aman's humming, and asked the reason for his happiness.

'Nothing. Just going to the temple with Riya,' Aman replied with a smile.

Kaalu made a face. 'Temple? That's your idea of a date?' He shook his head and leaned in. 'Come on, man. Want to celebrate for real?'

Aman smiled, amused. 'What do you mean by real?'

'My friends are meeting up—just for a bit. Chill time. You've earned a break.'

Aman hesitated. Riya's image flashed in his mind— waiting near the temple, dressed in white, glowing like always. But a voice inside whispered, *When was the last time you did something for yourself?*

Kaalu sensed the crack and pressed further. 'You study non-stop. Don't you deserve one hour to breathe?'

Aman's smile faded. Lately, even he had felt the weight building. Sleepless nights. Shaky hands during mocks. That one professor's voice still echoed: 'Stress is the real enemy.'

'I don't think it's a good idea,' Aman said. 'Riya's waiting...'

'She'll understand. One hour, Aman. That's all.'

And for once, Aman didn't resist. He looked at Kaalu—carefree, loose, unburdened—and felt a pang. *Maybe I'm missing out.* 'Alright,' he said softly. 'Just an hour.'

As they stepped into the car, Aman's fingers brushed against the keyring in Kaalu's hand. 'You've got the keys, right?'

Kaalu grinned. 'Relax, Mr Perfect. Of course.'

Aman smiled, but a sliver of unease settled in his gut.

～

The winter breeze grazed Aman's face as the car picked up speed. The music was loud, yet enchanting—romantic tracks flowing one after the other. 'Kora kagaz tha ye mann mera, likh diya naam us pe tera'—Lata ji and Kishore da's eternal classic. It was his favourite.

The chill in the air, the songs, the soft blur of city lights—it all made him miss Riya more than ever. His soul felt strangely elated, caught in that bittersweet pleasure of yearning. Sometimes, imagining a future with someone you love brings more warmth than their actual presence.

The car stopped outside a giant gate. A uniformed guard took down the number, the gates parted and they entered what looked like an elite enclave. A row of identical, exquisitely designed bungalows lined the lane. Each one looked like a dream. They parked and walked into one of them.

Aman stood speechless. It wasn't that he hadn't seen big houses before—his own haveli in Bikaner had thirteen rooms and a sprawling aangan. Their drawing hall alone had hosted dozens of ceremonies, from ring exchanges to sangeets. Nearly a hundred guests could sit in rows and eat together, no rented space ever needed. Their doors had always been open to friends and family. But this house was something else.

Unlike Aman's haveli, modern luxury poured from every corner of this bungalow. An L-shaped sofa with silk cushions embraced the living room. A grand dining table with throne-like chairs waited in elegance. A television stretched across the wall like a framed window and rich, abstract paintings hung with purpose. Chandelier lights bathed the room in hues of gold and amber. And outside, as if planted for pride—a glittering swimming pool.

Aman, still in awe, mumbled, 'Wow...this place is awesome.'

Kaalu beamed. 'Yeah. It is Vishal's. His dad's a big opposition leader.'

'Come, let me show you more,' Vishal said, leading them ahead.

They stepped into his personal room—an eclectic shrine to his passions. Posters of John Cena and The Undertaker stared down from one wall, Bryan Adams and the Backstreet Boys from another. A pool table anchored the space, flanked by a single bed and a study desk in opposite corners. A boxing bag swayed gently near the window; gloves and a sports bottle lay nearby. A guitar hung on a wall nail and sheets of musical notes were stuck to a polished white almirah. The room revealed a lot about its owner.

'Tea or coffee?' Vishal offered.

Aman declined. Kaalu and Rahul opted for coffee.

They all began to play Snooker. Vishal's shots were masterful; Rahul and Kaalu held their ground. But Aman, unexpectedly, proved to be a real contender—even though he hadn't played in years.

'Where'd you learn to play like that?' Vishal asked, genuinely impressed.

'There's a pool café in Bikaner,' Aman replied. 'Pay-and-play. I used to go there with friends. Picked up a thing or two.'

Kaalu watched quietly, a smile tugging at his lips. He often joked about Aman's old-school habits, but right now, he couldn't help feeling proud. His small-town friend was showing these big-city boys exactly what he was made of.

After a sweaty, high-spirited match, someone suggested a dip in the pool.

Aman checked his watch—he was running late. 'I really should go. Riya's waiting.'

But the others wouldn't hear of it.

'Just ten minutes,' Kaalu insisted. 'Come on, you've earned this.'

The water glistened. The idea of diving in, of letting go—just for a little while—was too tempting.

'I'll be quick,' Aman said, almost to himself.

They stripped down to boxers and sprinted into the pool, laughter echoing against the water. They swam like children, wild and free, tossing a ball and riding the high. Time slipped quietly by.

Suddenly, Aman realized that he was way too late. He scrambled out of the water, hurried to his clothes, reached for his phone—his heart dropped.

Twenty missed calls from Riya.

〜

Riya had been waiting outside Birla Temple for over an hour. The small box of peda in her hands had begun to sweat through its paper wrapping. She glanced again at her phone—twenty calls and no response.

A bead of frustration gathered on her temple. She wasn't one to anger easily, but this—this waiting—felt like a betrayal. Not because Aman was late, but because he hadn't bothered to inform her.

When the phone finally rang, she answered it.

'Riya...'

'Where are you, Aman?' Her voice was calm, dangerously so.

'I'm so sorry. I got caught up. I was with Kaalu and his friends. They dragged me into the pool—I lost track of time.'

Riya didn't respond for a moment. 'You lost track of time?'

'It's not what it sounds like. I didn't mean to—'

'Aman, I have been standing here. Alone. For two hours. No message, no heads-up. You knew how much this meant to me.' Her voice cracked. 'You knew I had made a promise...that I was going to offer prayers for you.'

Aman opened his mouth, then closed it. What excuse could make this better?

'I'm sorry,' he whispered. 'I messed up. Please...meet me in an hour outside my house. I'll explain everything. I'll be there. I promise.'

A long silence followed. It felt heavier than any scolding.

'Okay,' she said finally. 'I'll be there.'

As the call ended, for the first time Aman felt something unfamiliar twist inside him—shame.

Vishal noticed his change of expression. 'All okay?'

Aman sighed and recounted everything. How he'd gotten lost in the moment, how Riya had waited, how angry she'd been.

Kaalu scoffed from across the room. 'Yaar, she's being dramatic. You don't get to have fun every day—and she's upset? That's exactly why I don't do girlfriends.'

Aman shot back. 'She's not like that. She stood on the road alone for two hours, Kaalu. I should've called. That's on me.' He paused, turning serious. 'Anyway, I need to go now. Hand me the house keys.'

'Sure,' Kaalu replied casually. He checked his pant pockets. Then the back ones. Then the inner pocket of his boxers. His face shifted. 'They're not here.'

'What?' Aman blinked. 'Kaalu, I asked you to keep them safe.'

'I did! I mean... I thought I did.'

Aman's voice rose. 'You thought?'

Kaalu frowned. He didn't appreciate being yelled at, but this time, even he couldn't defend himself.

Rahul chimed in, 'Maybe they're in the car. Let's check.'

They all rushed down and searched the car thoroughly—under the seats, in the dashboard, everywhere. Nothing.

Vishal tried to ease the tension. 'Don't worry. You guys can stay here tonight. We'll sort out the keys tomorrow.'

Kaalu instantly accepted, almost too eagerly. But Aman's heart sank. He had promised Riya. And now there was no way to meet her without the keys—and, certainly, no time to explain this mess.

He called her again, voice low. 'Riya, I... I won't be able to meet you tonight. The house keys are lost. I'm stuck.'

There was silence on the other end. Then a sigh. 'It's okay,' she said, softer now. 'I understand.'

Aman hung up, disheartened. He didn't want to accept Vishal's hospitality, but there was no other choice.

Rahul offered to stay the night too. Vishal handed out pyjamas and soon the boys were all in casuals, snacks opened, music low, trying to revive the mood.

'Cheers to pyjama party!' Vishal announced.

There was popcorn, samosas, old VCDs and board games. Laughter echoed, but Aman's smile didn't quite reach his eyes. He tried to distract himself. Only when the warm spice of potato-pepper samosas filled his stomach did his heart calm a little.

Later, the boys sprawled around the bed. Aman felt a flicker of joy—he had always been unbeatable at board games. Maybe tonight wouldn't be so bad.

Then Kaalu pulled out a deck. 'Let's play something exciting,' he said, shuffling the cards. 'Money on the table.'

Aman blinked. 'Wait, we're gambling?'

Kaalu grinned. 'Come on, just one round. For fun.'

Aman stiffened. He had never gambled in his life. The very idea unsettled him.

'What the hell, Kaalu? Since when do you bet money?'

'Relax,' Rahul said, snapping his fingers at Aman. 'It's not that deep. Just play.'

Aman shook his head. 'I don't gamble. Never have.'

Rahul smirked and turned to Kaalu. 'Didn't know your friend's such a babu.'

Aman bristled. 'What do you mean by that?'

Before things could spiral, Vishal intervened. 'No one has to play if they don't want to.'

But Kaalu leaned in and whispered, 'Don't spoil the mood, yaar. Just one game. For me. Or I'll look bad.'

Aman gave in and placed his first bet. His luck was golden, just like his brain. One win followed another. He kept scooping up cash, the pile in front of him growing as the others laughed and cursed in jest. Eventually, they crowned him with a title—'The Fortune Master'.

The night grew darker. The stakes got higher. The thrill of winning tempted Aman to gamble more. But with each new bet, his luck faltered. Slowly, he began losing chunks of the money he'd earned and then more. A flicker of unease crept in.

Vishal poured him a glass of scotch. 'This'll lift you up.'

Aman hesitated. He had always been a teetotaller. But tonight, something in him wanted to rebel—against control, against restraint, against everything that had kept him 'good.' He gulped it down.

The spirit caught fire in his chest. The haze returned to his eyes, this time with a strange euphoria. The room tilted gently as the laughter grew louder. He drank again.

Then again. One more, for the high.

Soon, he wasn't Aman anymore—not the Aman who colour-coded his notes, who set alarms for mock tests, who counted how many calls Riya missed. That boy had been drowned in scotch and smoke.

For the first time, he felt like a teenager. Reckless. Weightless. Free.

Kaalu nudged him by the poolside, a half-lit cigarette between his fingers. 'Be honest. Don't you think you're carrying too much weight? You've missed out on your youth, Aman.'

Aman didn't answer.

Rahul grinned, tossing a pebble into the water. 'You must be dying to be in your girlfriend's bed right now, huh?'

Kaalu laughed before Aman could speak. 'No way. Their relationship isn't like that. I'm sure she hasn't even let him kiss her. No chance of sex.'

Aman stiffened. The insult jabbed deeper than the alcohol. 'That's not true,' he snapped. 'We've kissed. A bunch of times. And...we're planning to go further.'

'Oh please,' Kaalu scoffed. 'That arrogant girl? She's too full of herself. She doesn't even trust you.'

Something cracked inside Aman. 'I'll show you,' he shouted. 'I'll show you how much she wants to be in my arms.'

He'd lost all sense. No filter. No judgement. The night had consumed him.

When dawn finally crept in, the world still spinning slightly, Aman looked like he'd had the time of his life.

They returned to their room with a fresh set of keys and passed out in exhaustion.

The morning brought cornflakes without milk and reality without illusion.

Lazing on his bed, Aman checked his phone. Three missed calls from his mother. Four from friends. And more than a dozen from Riya.

He called her. Their conversation was normal—too normal. He skipped over the night entirely. But Riya sensed something had shifted. He was distant. Off-key. And that call ended, for the first time, without Aman saying 'Dhruv Tara.'

⌀

Life resumed. At least, it pretended to.

Aman immersed himself in books, numbers and statistics. It helped him avoid people. Avoid thoughts. Kaalu, meanwhile, showed up to classes but spent most days at the movies or with friends, ignoring his studies altogether.

One day, Aman finally confronted him. 'You need to take this seriously,' he said. 'Competition's brutal. You're not prepared.'

Kaalu laughed in response. 'And you are? Slogging day and night just to go back and sell laddoos at your father's shop?'

Aman stared at him.

'Let me get this straight,' Kaalu continued, voice rising. 'You want a top college degree just to become a halwai? Just to go back to that cramped little town where the entire neighbourhood knows when you sneeze? You could build something real here. But you're too scared.' He paused, then added, 'Maybe that's your problem—you're physically here, but your mind is stuck in the past. You're still that backward boy too afraid to live in a big city.'

Aman had no answer. His world wobbled under his feet.

He thought of Riya, of how things had changed. They spoke less now. Their calls were shorter, colder. Since that night, an awkward distance had settled between them. And the worst part? Aman didn't even know how to undo it.

His mind was restless. The syllabus felt heavier than ever. His heart felt hollow.

Kaalu noticed the turmoil, though he didn't say much. He had problems of his own. His funds from home were drying up—drained by impulsive spending and a growing list of vices.

Then came an invitation from Rahul—a party. Loud, wild, numbing. A candle in their growing darkness.

Kaalu jumped at it, dragging Aman along.

'Come on,' he said. 'Unwind. Let go.'

And Aman agreed. He needed to breathe. Needed to forget.

Kaalu picked out a peppy T-shirt for him—brighter than Aman would ever wear. But tonight, nothing felt off-limits.

The party was everything Aman once avoided—

booze, smoke, loud girls, louder boys. At first, it felt strange. Then it felt freeing. Then it felt like truth.

He wanted to let go of the fear. The fear that no matter how hard he tried, he'd always end up back where he started. He lifted his first glass and raised a toast. 'To the reincarnated Aman.'

The lion had tasted blood. And he didn't stop drinking till it burned. The only thing that buzzed in his mind was simple: live your youth to the fullest.

The party had faded into a haze. Aman, now on his fourth drink, sat on the edge of the balcony, legs dangling, his body humming with a heady mix of scotch, smoke and a kind of emptiness that wasn't entirely new— but had never felt this loud.

Around him, laughter buzzed like static. Vishal was pouring another drink, Kaalu had disappeared with someone's Bluetooth speaker and Rahul was mid-rant about girls who 'played hard to get'.

Aman's phone buzzed. It was 1:47 a.m.

He scrolled through his messages, thumb hovering over Riya's name. Her last text blinked up at him: 'Hope you ate something. Good night.'

His fingers dialled her before his mind could catch up.

'Aman?' Her voice was groggy. 'Is everything okay?'

He smiled faintly. 'I miss you.'

A pause. 'I've missed you too,' she said gently. 'You've been…distant lately. I didn't know if I should call.'

'You should've,' he whispered. 'I needed to hear your voice.'

'I'm glad you called.' She hesitated. 'Are you—are you drinking?'

'Maybe.' A laugh escaped him. 'Don't worry, it's just a little celebration. My mind's been heavy. I needed to let go for once.'

'Is that why you've been avoiding me?'

Her voice wasn't angry—just vulnerable. He hated that.

'No, not really... I just...' He took a breath. 'Riya, can I ask you something?'

'Of course.'

'Have you ever thought about us...you know... taking things further?'

Silence.

He pressed on, too far gone to stop. 'Like, being closer. Physically. Not just emotionally.'

'Aman—'

'Don't freak out. I'm just asking. Don't you think it's normal? We're in love. We've been together for years. Why not?'

Her breath hitched. 'Because that's not us. And this—this isn't you.'

He laughed again, but it was bitter now. 'Maybe you don't trust me enough. Maybe you never have.'

That cut through her. 'How can you say that?'

'Because if you did, you wouldn't assume the worst every time I bring up something real.'

'No,' she said quietly, 'I think the worst because this doesn't feel real. You sound like someone else. Someone who doesn't care how I feel.'

Aman swallowed. He wanted to take it back, but, instead, he said the one thing he shouldn't: 'Maybe you're just scared. Scared to love without rules.'

'And maybe,' she replied, voice steady, 'you're just scared to be loved without being in control.'

The line went dead.

Aman stared at his screen. His head spun and his chest felt heavier than it had in months.

ॐ

A lot changed after that.

Riya stopped reaching out. Aman embraced the version of himself he had once judged. His clothes changed and so did his identity. He was seen less in classrooms and more in movie theatres. His marks slipped. His circle shifted. New addictions took root.

He stopped looking forward to vacations.

Going home meant facing people who would see the truth. It meant explaining this new version of himself to people who remembered the old one. Still, he had no choice. He returned.

His parents were surprised. His mother's eyes welled up as she hugged him. He was welcomed like a dignitary. And somehow, that only made him feel worse. He rushed to his room.

At dinner, his father tried light conversation. 'Why the earrings? And...those clothes?'

Aman shrugged. 'It's fashion. That's how guys dress in the city now.'

His mother gently interrupted his father's reply. 'Don't judge his appearance,' she said. 'The city must be hard to survive.'

Days passed and the glow of his return wore off. His parents began to notice the shift—the absence in his eyes, the edge in his voice. They'd already heard about his poor performance through whispers and warnings from teachers.

His mother caught a quiet moment and spoke gently. 'I won't ask you why your marks have dropped. Or why your attitude feels different. I just want to say one thing—this is the golden time of your life. The years that shape your future. If you let it slip away, it won't come back. You'll only be left with regret.'

To Aman, it felt like a lecture. He bristled. 'Yes,' he snapped. 'It is golden. That's why I won't compromise it for some distant, hollow future.'

She didn't understand the exact meaning of his words, but she understood the pain behind them.

The next day, his father asked him to visit the shop. 'Just see it once,' he said. 'Come watch what it means to run something generations have built.'

'I'm not joining the halwai clan,' Aman said flatly, retreating to his room.

His father stood there, deeply hurt, but silent. Some battles, he knew, couldn't be won by arguing.

The next day, Aman prepared to return to the city. Before he left, he stepped toward his father for a brief goodbye.

But his father didn't let it be brief. He pulled Aman

into a firm embrace and said quietly, 'The day I sent you away to study, I was prepared. I knew the world outside would change you. It wasn't easy for us, but we never wanted you to be a frog in a well. We gave you wings because we believed—an apple doesn't fall far from the tree.'

He paused and looked into Aman's eyes. 'I understand you may not want to come back and sit in the sweet shop. That's why I've already bought a piece of land for you. You can open a hotel, a café, even a restaurant— whatever you dream of. We'll run a branch of our sweet shop there too, if you like. Bring your own ideas, give our legacy a new direction.'

He meant every word. Aman could see it. And yet, he said nothing.

He left without a single reply, which ripped something inside his parents. They didn't show it. But they felt it.

Neither his mother's gentle warnings nor his father's loving vision could snap him out of the haze. But one thing did: fear. He resolved, silently, to start studying again—not out of clarity or motivation, but simply to avoid failing. Avoid being called back home in shame.

~

Aman opened his inbox. Two new emails waited.

The first, from the admin office: 'Dear Student, your attendance in the following subjects is below the mandatory threshold.'

The second, from the finance department: 'Your

next tuition instalment is due. Failure to pay may result in an academic block.'

His chest tightened. He hadn't realized things had gotten this bad.

He opened his bank app for the first time in weeks. The screen blinked: ₹113.

Panicked, he texted his father: 'Need ₹3,000 urgently—for materials and food.'

Two hours later, the reply came. 'Son, we just paid your hostel and tuition. Let's talk next week.'

He stared at the screen. His throat went dry.

Calling Riya wasn't an option. Not after everything. Not like this.

Kaalu, noticing his state, offered a solution. 'You want money? Do what I do.'

Aman hesitated. 'What...do you do?'

Kaalu only grinned.

With no better choice, Aman followed.

∽

The next evening, they stood outside a bustling movie theatre.

It was Aman's first brush with street hustling. They arrived early, bought a handful of tickets before the counter opened and waited. As the crowd thickened, they began reselling—to those who didn't want to wait in line.

By the time the shutters closed, desperation filled the air. Kaalu hiked up prices and they made good money.

It was time to celebrate Aman's first earning.

Next day wasn't any different. The sun had barely begun to set when Aman and Kaalu reached the gates of Regal Cinema. The posters of a new blockbuster flapped against the walls and the faint smell of roasted peanuts wafted through the air.

Aman stood beside Kaalu, a wad of tickets tucked nervously in his shirt pocket. The crowd was swelling. The official counter wouldn't open for another hour.

'Today's the day we score big,' Kaalu whispered, eyes gleaming. 'Just follow my lead. Don't overthink.'

Aman nodded but his heart thudded in protest. Each minute felt like he was chiselling away at a version of himself he didn't recognize anymore.

People passed, some pausing, some bargaining, some walking off. A few tickets got sold. But nothing great. Aman was just about to suggest they pack up and leave when Kaalu nudged him hard.

'Them. Go. Now.'

A sharply dressed woman in a red sari was walking toward the box office with a tall man in a crisp shirt and sunglasses. They reached just as the shutter clanged down.

'Perfect,' Kaalu whispered. 'Go to them. Quote high. We need this one.'

Aman hesitated. 'What if they say no?'

'Then charm them. You've got that face. Just go.'

Swallowing his pride, Aman walked over. 'Excuse me, sir. The counter's closed, but I've got two tickets. Decent seats. If you're interested…'

The man raised an eyebrow. 'How much?'

Aman glanced back at Kaalu, then named a price—double the original.

'Excuse me?' the man snapped. 'Double?'

'It's negotiable,' Aman said, trying to stay calm. 'Just that they're the last two…'

'You think we're fools?' the man's voice rose. 'This is theft, not resale. You leech off people's desperation. People like you ruin everything.'

A crowd began to form, attracted by the raised voice. Aman's ears turned hot. He looked around for Kaalu but couldn't see him.

The man jabbed a finger in Aman's chest. 'What's your name? You think wearing jeans makes you untouchable? You're nothing but a thief.'

Then came the slap—sharp, open-palmed, across Aman's cheek. A gasp escaped the crowd.

Aman staggered back, clutching his face, stunned more by the words than the sting. 'I swear…this isn't who I am,' he stammered. 'I'm a student. From a good family. This is—this was just—'

The man scoffed. 'You expect me to believe that? Look at you.'

Aman's breath caught. For the first time, he actually looked at himself—greasy hair, faded jeans, a tee with a cracked print that read 'Thug Life'. He looked like exactly what the man had called him.

The woman touched the man's arm. 'Let it go. Let's not ruin our evening. He's just a boy.'

The man muttered something under his breath and

turned away. The crowd dispersed slowly.

Aman stood frozen, the weight of every bad choice bearing down on him like concrete. Then, from a distance, he saw Kaalu—half-hidden behind a pillar, watching.

Their eyes met. Kaalu turned and disappeared.

Aman didn't move for a long time. When he finally walked away, he did so with his head down, hands trembling, shame staining every step. The air around him felt thick. Dirty.

That night, he couldn't eat. Couldn't sleep. Kaalu offered him water, jokes, even music. Aman didn't respond. He stared at the ceiling, the man's words echoing in his mind: 'You expect me to believe that? Look at you.'

For the first time, Aman believed them.

He realized how far he had drifted. From shirts and trousers to vulgar T-shirts and torn jeans. From using every minute wisely to killing time without purpose. From ambition to apathy. From being a teetotaller to a drunk. From a cherished son and devoted boyfriend to someone forgotten, forsaken. He was lost—right in the middle of nowhere.

Kaalu slept soundly on the other bed, unbothered. Aman stared at him. How could he rest so peacefully after what had happened? There was no shame on his face. No remorse. No hint of guilt.

Aman's thoughts churned. He ran when I needed him most. Vanished into the shadows while I stood alone in a crowd, being slapped by a stranger. Perhaps he's always been like that. Perhaps I always knew. I just chose to forget.

His mind wouldn't stop.

We were always poles apart. I never admired his ways. I saw through him—his laziness, his vices, his lack of drive. I used to tell him to work harder, aim higher. But today...today there's no difference between us.

He couldn't rise to my level, so he pulled me down to his. Bit by bit, I stopped being me. I became more like him.

The irony burned.

We're so quick to envy others' lives without realizing they might envy ours. We dream of stepping into someone else's shoes without appreciating our own. And when we don't know how hard another person's life really is, maybe the smarter thing is to walk on our own and walk proudly.

It's better to have an enemy who slaps you in the face than a friend who stabs you in the back.

His mother's voice echoed in his ears: 'If you let this golden time slip away, it will never come back.'

Each word struck deeper now. How right she had been.

He thought of his father—how he had belittled their family's legacy. The pride that came from running a generations-old sweet shop, from making their name a delicacy known even to foreign tourists. His father had carried that with grace.

And he—he had treated it like dust.

He couldn't think of Riya. That pain was too sharp,

too fresh. He had wounded the most precious girl in his life. His bruises were nothing compared to what he had done to her trust. The way he mocked her love. The way he made her feel unsafe in what should have been their sanctuary.

He wanted to rewind time. To go back. Undo everything. But life, cruelly, has no rewind button. No pause. He was choking just being in the same room as Kaalu. But he knew stepping out wouldn't fix what was inside him. So, he took a breath. And left the house.

Sometimes in life, we stumble. We fall. We lose our balance. But what matters is the courage to rise again.

He didn't know what waited ahead. He couldn't see the full staircase. But he took the first step.

Across the city, her phone buzzed beneath her pillow. And Riya didn't miss his call.

9

Better than Perfect

When you are isolated, you realize what being with people means. It's so easy to think we need no one, that we're complete on our own—but is that really true?

In Bollywood movies, two lovers often run away from their homes, their families, their cities, just to be together. They start living in isolation, with each other, for each other, away from everything. No one else to talk to, laugh with, or lean on—and apparently, they need no one. It's funny because that's where the movie ends. They never show what comes after.

But the 2020 quarantine did. It showed what happens when people are truly isolated. Couples dreaded the idea that they might end up fighting non-stop if forced to stay indoors together. Some even joked about nightmares in which they were literally killing each other. People missed crowds, conversations, companionship. The hum of the outside world.

Emotionally, physically, mentally—in every way, humans need humans. Without people, there's nothing to look forward to. No interaction, no competition, no motivation. It became a phase of realization. A time to ask: where on earth are we the safest? Of course—our own homes. But when people were bugged to no limits, when everything outside was locked and all interactions cut off—yes, that was the time of COVID-19.

It was then that Raghu began noticing the real story—the one that usually starts after the curtain falls. A passionate filmmaker at heart, he had always been drawn to what lay beneath the polished surface, and now, he was seeing it unfold in his own life.

Reena and Raghu—names that feel straight out of a feel-good film—seemed to be everything a modern couple aspired to be. They looked happy, in sync and utterly in love. Every couple around admired them. Some even envied them.

Reena, tall and lean with a dusky glow, was Raghu's apple of the eye. Short, plump, fair Raghu was everything Reena had ever dreamt of. Reena was neither a housewife nor a conventional professional. In today's terms, she was a 'mompreneur'—full-time mom, part-time blogger. She was always busy, juggling her roles as mother, wife and content creator. Her Instagram stories of a happy family—with her twinning baby and ever-smiling husband—were loved by all. Their social media showcased them as the epitome of happiness. But behind the filters and captions, like in any household, there were moments undocumented.

No, don't over-assume. There are no dark secrets behind their pictures. There's no twist coming that reveals it was all fake. Their smiles, their setup—it was real. They truly loved each other. But, like any couple, there were things they didn't say out loud.

They had never fought—at least not the way most couples do. They lived in balance, harmony, a kind of quiet understanding. But that doesn't mean there weren't unspoken things. Sometimes, Reena paused a second too long in the mirror, wondering if her smile in the photo felt more staged than sincere. Raghu, some nights, wished he could dig into his dinner without pausing for a picture. But they moved on. Because they cared and because their life had rhythm.

Reena's ideal day began early: cooking breakfast, dropping her son to school, managing the house, doing her puja and then heading off to her bloggers' meet. Later, she'd pick up her son, help with homework, hit the gym, click her pictures of the day and by the time Raghu got home, they'd be off to some club or social gathering. After dinner, it was time for bed—tired but content.

Raghu's ideal day began with squash or swimming, then breakfast, then work. He pushed hard to be noticed, to get promoted. Evenings were for playtime with his son, the daily picture with Reena and then another round of socializing—just so they didn't feel left out of the world.

Then came the lockdown. Like a thunderclap.

Suddenly, no offices, no clubs, no outings. The world froze. Everyone was locked indoors, with only their families for company. The assumption was—our ideal couple, Reena and Raghu, would handle it the best. If anything, they'd give us major goals for how to thrive during quarantine.

For the first time, Reena and Raghu were together all day, every day. No distractions, no duties pulling them away.

'This is so nice,' Raghu said, sipping his evening tea on Day One. 'We finally have time together.'

Reena nodded. 'No rushing. No traffic. Just us.'

And for a few days, it was indeed nice. They cooked together, watched movies, played games with their son. Reena updated her stories with cheerful hashtags like #QuarantineDiaries. Raghu smiled through the posed selfies, even when she asked for second or third takes.

But gradually, the calm started stretching too thin. The quiet that once felt peaceful began to echo. There were no blogger meets for Reena to attend, no work calls for Raghu to retreat into. Their days, once perfectly scheduled, now spilt into each other.

'Do you miss the parties?' Raghu asked one afternoon as they lounged on the balcony.

'Honestly?' Reena hesitated. 'Not really. I never liked them much.'

He looked at her, surprised. 'What do you mean? You always looked like you were having fun.'

She sighed. 'I smiled for the camera. But most of the time, I felt out of place. I hated the noise—the shallow conversations, the backhanded compliments, the performative friendships. Drunk men, showbiz gossip, fake laughs—it always drained me. I went because you loved them.'

Raghu was stunned. 'I didn't know you felt that way.'

'I didn't say anything,' she said quietly. 'You seemed so at home in those spaces. I didn't want to dampen your mood.'

A strange heaviness settled between them. The kind that comes not from disagreement, but from suddenly realizing how much one didn't know about the person they live with.

The next day, to pass the time, Reena suggested they bake a cake together. 'It'll be fun,' she said, tousling her son's hair. 'We haven't done this in ages.'

Raghu agreed, albeit with a shrug. Their son clapped with excitement. For the next hour, flour dusted the kitchen tiles, eggshells cracked imperfectly and laughter filled the air like the scent of vanilla.

When the cake was finally out of the oven, golden and perfect, Raghu and their son stood ready—forks in hand, wide-eyed and hungry.

'Attack!' Raghu declared, raising his fork like a warrior.

'Wait!' Reena interjected. 'I need a picture of the cake. For the story. It'll look incomplete without the final shot.'

Raghu paused mid-motion. Then, slowly lowered his fork.

'Reena...' he said, not smiling anymore. 'Can we just

eat the cake? Just this once, without clicking?'

She looked surprised. 'It'll only take a second.'

'It's never just a second,' he snapped. 'It's always a pose. A filter. A caption. Every damn time.'

She blinked. 'What's that supposed to mean?'

'It means I'm tired,' Raghu said. 'Tired of pretending I enjoy it. Tired of waiting to eat because the light isn't perfect. Tired of dressing up like a prop in your digital gallery. I've never said it, but I hate it, Reena. I hate how everything is for show.'

She stared at him. 'Then why didn't you ever say anything? Why pretend to be the perfect husband if it was all a lie?'

'Because I thought it made you happy. And maybe it did, in the beginning. But now...now it feels like you're living more for your followers than for us. You've forgotten the line between private and public.'

She looked away, her hands trembling slightly as she set the phone down. 'You think I'm fake?'

'I think,' he said carefully, 'you've lost sight of where the performance ends. You used to live the moment and then share it. Now I feel like you only live it so you can share it.'

They didn't realize how loud they had gotten—until their five-year-old started clapping.

They turned, confused.

'Why are you clapping?' Raghu asked.

The boy beamed. 'Because now I get to say, "Mumma, Papa, don't fight!" Then you'll hug me, like Aarav's parents!'

They stared at him, stunned. The absurdity, the innocence, the sharp contrast between his joy and their tension—something about it cracked them open. Raghu chuckled, a dry sound that turned into a quiet laugh. Reena covered her mouth, blinking back tears, and nodded.

Later that night, after their son had fallen asleep, Reena and Raghu sat in silence, the cake still untouched. The kitchen lights cast a soft glow—warm, unfiltered, real.

'We fought today,' Reena said, her voice quiet.

Raghu gave a slow nod. 'For the first time.'

'But it didn't break us.'

'It opened something,' he said. 'Like we remembered how to be honest again.'

She took a breath. 'Perhaps we needed that. We've spent so much time trying to be a perfect picture... maybe we forgot how to be a real story.'

Their son stirred and muttered something incoherent. Reena rose, tucked him in and returned. Raghu lit a candle—an old one they used to light during power cuts. Its flame danced, quiet and unapologetic.

This is what house arrest had done to them. This is what happens when the noise outside fades and people are left alone with themselves. This is what quarantine brings—not just irritation and confinement, but truth.

Sometimes, people stay so busy, they forget to touch the deeper chords. Going with the flow feels easier than pausing to feel. Isolation gave them that pause—to be frustrated, to fight. And to finally speak.

Thanks to COVID-19 and quarantine, Reena and Raghu may no longer look perfect in their Instagram stories, but in the truest sense, their relationship has become a real one.

Better than perfect, one might say.

10

The God Within

At thirteen, I was unusually curious—so curious, in fact, that my grandmother started calling me 'Prashanna', a name she gave me for my ever-questioning mind.

'It suits you,' she'd say with a soft chuckle, patting my head after yet another barrage of questions over breakfast.

I remember one Diwali evening, watching Grandma light the diyas with quiet devotion. The air smelled of marigolds and ghee, the walls glowed with flickering flames and the house buzzed with whispered prayers. But even then, my mind stirred restlessly.

'If God is everywhere,' I had asked her softly, 'why do we need to light lamps to find Him?'

She smiled and said, 'Because, beta, sometimes even God likes a warm welcome.'

I nodded, but the answer nestled into a corner of my mind—unsettled, unanswered. Even as I joined in the prayers, a small part of me stood apart, wondering if faith was more about ritual than truth.

I asked questions not just because I was curious, but because I couldn't help myself. Sometimes, at school, friends would argue over whose god was real, whose prayers worked better. I'd listen quietly, wondering why faith needed sides at all. It was the way my mind worked—always turning things over, peering underneath, tugging at loose threads.

I read strange facts online, watched space documentaries late into the night, and once genuinely wondered aloud why no one ever asked questions about mythology the way they did about science. With answers always just a swipe away, I'd grown up expecting explanations, not instructions. And in a world where identities were often divided by faith, I found myself drawn instead to what felt real—kindness, thoughtfulness, truth.

I wasn't the kind of child who did things just because I was told to. I needed reasons, explanations, the why behind everything. And growing up in a home where almost every religion in India had found its place, there were plenty of questions to ask.

My family was a tapestry of faiths and beliefs. Grandma, a devout Hindu, had married my quiet, philosophical Muslim grandfather. When my father brought home my mother—born into a Sikh family—they welcomed her into their eclectic household without hesitation. And so,

I was raised in an environment that never forced a label on me. I grew up hearing shlokas, namaz and gurbani under the same roof—each melody weaving into my life like threads of a single song.

One mild Sunday morning, with the smell of cardamom tea in the air, Grandma called out, 'Chalo beta, get ready. We're going to the temple.'

I looked up from my sketchbook and, without much thought, said, 'I don't want to go.'

She paused, her wrinkled hands frozen mid-fold in her sari pleats. 'Why not?' she asked, more surprised than upset.

'I don't think I ever want to go to the temple,' I replied honestly.

A longer pause followed. She set her tea cup down. 'Do you want to go to the mosque instead?'

'No,' I shook my head.

She looked at me carefully, as if trying to read the space between my words. 'Gurdwara?' she asked gently, her voice full of hope.

I hesitated, then said, 'No, not that either.'

By now, the entire family was listening. My mother dropped a ladle into the sink. My father raised his newspaper a little too sharply. Even Dadaji adjusted his glasses, squinting at me from over their rim.

'I don't understand where God stays,' I explained, trying to keep my voice steady. 'If He's in the temple, then why the mosque? And if He's in the mosque, why the gurdwara? And if He's everywhere, then...why go anywhere?'

The silence that followed was deafening. My father's jaw tightened. My mother looked at me like I'd just confessed to a crime. I wanted to run, hide, vanish into the folds of our heavy velvet curtains. But somewhere beneath the anxiety, I felt something warm—something like pride.

I had asked a question no one could answer.

Grandma broke the tension. 'Let's all take a little break,' she said calmly. 'Meet me in the drawing room in ten minutes—with tea. Even bold questions deserve good chai.'

We gathered around the old leather-polished wooden table—worn with years of family debates and bedtime stories. The steam from the cups curled like incense in the air, and despite the tension, something about tea always made things better.

Grandma began, 'First, I want to say…I'm proud of you. It's brave to question what everyone just accepts.'

Dadaji stirred his tea slowly. 'You know,' he said, his voice like sandpaper softened by time, 'the Quran doesn't ask us to follow blindly either. Iqra—the very first word revealed—means "read". Understand. Reflect. Faith should never come without thought.'

Maa looked over from her cup, her expression gentler now. 'When I was your age, I once refused to tie my hair before entering the gurdwara. I didn't understand why it mattered. But over time, I learnt that sometimes rituals help us quiet our minds—even if we don't understand them fully at first.'

My father stayed quiet, sipping his tea slowly. But I caught the flicker of a smile behind the newspaper, as if something in him had eased. The knot in my chest loosened just a little.

Grandma leaned in, her voice soft yet steady. 'Let me tell you a story I once heard—one I've never forgotten.'

Then she looked at me directly. 'Long ago, when the world was still learning how to be human, God and the Devil had a terrible fight. Both wanted to rule over mankind—body, mind and soul.

'"Let me lead them," said the Devil. "I can make them powerful, greedy, cunning."

'"No," said God, "they deserve light, truth and love."

'They fought for days, nights, years—until time itself gave up counting. Finally, they struck a deal.

'"Let us not fight anymore," said God. "We shall let humans decide. When they think good thoughts, I will live in them. And when they choose bad, the Devil can have them."

'And so it was done. No temples, no mosques, no statues or symbols. Just thoughts. Just choices. Just the soul.'

I stared at her, my tea forgotten. Something about that story cracked open a door inside me.

She smiled, her eyes glinting with wisdom. 'So you see, beta, God doesn't live in temples or mosques or gurdwaras. He lives inside you. He awakens with your kindness, your honesty, your courage. When you think good thoughts, you bring Him alive.'

There was a stillness in the room, the kind that happens when truth settles in.

◡◦

The God Within

Later that month, I went to the gurdwara with Maa. The stream of water at the entrance washed over my feet like a quiet blessing and as I stepped inside, the steady rhythm of gurbani wrapped around me like a song I didn't need to understand to feel. I cupped the holy water and sprinkled it gently over my head. In the langar, rolling up my sleeves to serve steaming food on steel plates, I felt a joy I couldn't explain—something sacred in giving, something divine in doing.

That night, I sat alone in my room, the scent of lentils still clinging to my sleeves. I didn't know what I believed in exactly, but something inside me had shifted. Maybe truth didn't always arrive with fireworks—maybe it tiptoed in through acts of kindness, through the rhythm of shared silence.

A few days later, I found myself waking early with Dadaji. The mosque was quiet at dawn, wrapped in stillness. I watched people bow low to the ground, their foreheads pressed to the marble. The call to prayer rang out—not loud, but deep, resonant. Allahu Akbar. The words seemed to sweep through the arches and into the soul, reducing pride, shrinking ego. There was no space for judgment here—only surrender. The quiet rhythm of prayer felt like the heartbeat of the universe.

Afterwards, Dadaji handed me a date and smiled. 'Submission isn't weakness,' he said. 'It's the courage to let go of control.'

I didn't reply, but I tucked his words away like a pebble in my pocket—smooth, grounding.

One evening, after a long day of homework and

half-finished sketches, I walked with Grandma to the temple she loved so much. The scent of sandalwood lingered in the air, mingling with jasmine and the faint ring of temple bells. A small shrine beside the sanctum echoed with chants of 'Govinda Govinda', and the idol of Krishna smiled with a playful mischief. I watched as volunteers helped the disabled up the steps, fed the poor and offered shelter—not just prayers.

On the wall near the altar, I read an inscription: 'हे नाथ, मैं आपको भूलूँ नही'—O Lord, I will never forget you. Those words didn't demand devotion. They invited remembrance. Not of rules, but of goodness.

From that day on, I stopped worrying about where I should go to find God. Instead, I began noticing Him—in small moments. In helping Maa with dishes without being asked. In forgiving a friend who broke my trust. In choosing kindness when it would've been easier to be cruel.

Sometimes I still go to the temple with Grandma. Other times I sit quietly in the gurdwara or listen to Dadaji's verses as the sun rises slow and golden through our window.

I don't feel the need to choose anymore—not between places or names or paths. Because, perhaps, the question wasn't where God lived. Maybe it was whether I left enough room for Him to stay.

People still ask me, 'What religion do you follow?'

I smile and say, 'The one that teaches me to think good thoughts. The one that helps me keep God within.'

11

....

Terms and Conditions Applied

On a warm summer afternoon, Pushkar sat perched on a high bar stool at Rock Café in Goa, a half-finished Scotch and soda resting on the counter beside him. The swimming pool shimmered just ahead, echoing with the laughter of parents and the excited shrieks of children. He looked on with a faint smile, one which didn't reach his eyes.

Goa had always been his escape—a sacred getaway he made twice a year, religiously, with his gang of college friends. But this time, the barstool next to him was empty. One by one, his friends had given in to marriage and domesticity, and this year even the last bachelor among them had surrendered to the inevitable.

They'd promised a final all-boys trip—'one for the road', as Pushkar called it—but that plan fizzled out like an unopened beer can in the sun. No one wanted to leave their wives, and no one wanted to argue. Disappointed but determined, Pushkar had come alone. It was, after all, a good time for a solo trip—or so he'd told himself.

He worked as a financial planner at a prestigious UK-based bank, heading their Indian operations from Indore. The perks were exceptional—an envious salary, paid vacations, a lifestyle many of his peers only dreamt of. Twice a year, the bank offered fully funded holidays, one domestic and one international. With his relentless deadlines and the constant pressure of targets, these breaks weren't just a luxury—they were a lifeline.

But that day, the buzz of Goa didn't quite lift his spirits the way it used to. He sipped his drink and let the Scotch burn gently down his throat. He'd always imagined solo travel would feel liberating—just like in the Hollywood movies he loved watching growing up. Instead, it felt hollow. He missed the noise of familiar voices, the inside jokes, the late-night beach talks with his friends. It hit him in that moment—fun, real fun, was rarely about the place. It was about people.

A flicker of loneliness stirred in him—not the kind that comes from being alone, but the kind that comes from not having someone to share your silences with. On impulse, he borrowed a pen from the bartender and flipped open his small diary. It had been months since he had last written in it. He thought he'd try to shape his restlessness into a poem—or at least a note to himself.

Pushkar hailed from a traditional Gujarati family—close-knit, business-minded and deeply rooted in cultural values. At thirty, he had become the subject of constant matchmaking efforts by his parents and relatives.

'Before it's too late,' his mother would say over dinner, while his father forwarded yet another bio-data on WhatsApp.

For years, he'd dodged these pressures with ease. He wanted to enjoy his freedom—his late-night drives, spontaneous getaways, quiet cups of tea with no one to answer to. But now, the thrill of being untethered had dulled. The idea of companionship had begun to warm on him. For the first time in his life, he found himself not resisting the thought of marriage.

He liked to think of himself as broadminded, different from the usual matrimonial checklist. He didn't demand dowry or expect a wife to give up her career. He'd told himself he was progressive. Open. Flexible.

But there was one belief he wasn't ready to let go of—a decision that had become his life's most controversial clause.

He didn't want children. Not now. Not ever.

It wasn't that he disliked them. But the idea of parenting felt alien to him. He had never seen himself as a father—never imagined himself rocking a baby to sleep or chasing toddlers around a living room. He wasn't wired that way. And more than that, he questioned the very premise of it all.

'Why should I bring someone into the world if I

don't feel called to raise them?' he would ask, more to himself than anyone else.

For Pushkar, life wasn't about legacy—it was about experience. He wanted to drink every drop of it, not spend it worrying about school admissions, vaccinations or tuition fees. He didn't see it as selfish; he saw it as honest.

But honesty had its price. Most women he dated assumed he would eventually change his mind. When he didn't, the relationships unravelled—sometimes with quiet sadness, sometimes with rage. His family found his stance baffling.

'This isn't how life works,' his aunt once snapped. 'Marriage means family. Family means children.'

Pushkar didn't argue anymore. He knew what he wanted. And more importantly, he knew what he couldn't offer. He wasn't out to change anyone's dreams. He simply hoped to find someone whose dreams aligned with his.

At the poolside bar, the din of squealing children snapped him out of his thoughts. He looked around—the clamour of tiny voices, the splashes, the repeated 'Papa! Mumma!' echoing in the air. He stirred uncomfortably in his seat.

A toddler threw a tantrum nearby and a juice glass toppled over. He sighed, lifting his drink closer to his ears as if to drown the noise. Even Rihanna's bold voice couldn't rise above the chaos.

He took one last sip and was about to move to a quieter spot when he saw her.

She moved with the quiet confidence of someone comfortable in her skin. A white crochet shrug fell loosely over a red swimsuit, and her mahogany-red hair was tied in a casual knot, wisps dancing in the sea breeze. She slid on to the stool beside him and signalled the bartender with a practiced ease, ordering a mojito in a voice as crisp as the drink itself.

Pushkar noticed her in profile first—a graceful jawline, almond-shaped eyes scanning the bar, a small crease forming between her brows as she caught him staring.

Busted.

He flinched, almost childishly, then attempted to recover. 'I, uh—sorry. I get nervous around pretty women,' he offered, half-smile and all.

She turned to face him, lips curling. 'That's unfortunate. I know a few better opening lines—if you're open to notes.'

They both laughed. The awkwardness broke, just like that.

'I'm Hetal,' she said, holding out her hand.

'Pushkar,' he replied, still surprised to hear a name so rooted in home, spoken in an accent so effortless and modern.

They clinked glasses. Conversation followed. What began as small talk—Goa, travel, music—soon spiralled into a flowing rhythm. Time folded into itself. The sun began its slow descent behind the palms and dusk painted the sky in deep lavender as they talked about cities, careers, family expectations and the quiet rebellion of choosing one's own path.

Hetal told him she was a doctor—born and raised in Ahmedabad, now pursuing her master's degree in California after completing her MBBS. She had come to India for her brother's wedding and decided to extend her stay in Goa for a few days of solitude before flying back.

He found himself leaning in, not just out of attraction but intrigue. She was sharp, articulate and unapologetically ambitious.

'And you?' she asked.

'I head the India branch of a UK-based bank,' Pushkar replied. 'Though I dream of leaving it all behind and joining my family's tea business some day.'

'What's stopping you?' Hetal's asked, curious.

'Big salaries and bigger perks,' he sheepishly replied. 'They are like sugar traps. You get hooked before you know it.'

She nodded with understanding. 'My brother says the same. Golden cages are still cages.'

Pushkar looked at her, surprised. Few people got that.

And just like that, the gap between them didn't feel so wide anymore.

Later that evening, as the crowd around them thickened and music pulsed louder from the beachside speakers, they moved to a quieter corner of the café patio. Pushkar had always liked talking, but he was surprised by how much he liked listening.

Hetal sipped slowly on her third mojito, her gaze tracing the sky as it deepened into blue.

'There's something I don't usually tell people,' she said, her tone softening.

Pushkar waited.

'My mother died of breast cancer when I was fourteen.'

The words were plain, but the silence that followed said everything else. He didn't speak—just nodded, letting her continue.

'It was quick and cruel. We tried everything—top hospitals, specialists, prayers. But back then, detection came late and options were limited. No one really talked about oncology the way they do now. We didn't even know what to look for.'

She paused, staring at the condensation on her glass.

'I didn't eat for weeks. Didn't speak to anyone. Then one day, I saw my father crying in the kitchen—trying to hide it, failing. That broke something inside me.'

Her voice grew steadier, more focused.

'That's when I decided I'd become a doctor. Not just for her, but for every family that feels helpless in hospital corridors. I worked my way through med school in Ahmedabad, and now I'm doing my MS in California. Oncology is my endgame. I want to return to India once I've trained enough—build something that lasts.'

She paused for a moment, then added, 'But that won't happen soon. I've got years of training ahead—and I need to stay in the US for all of it. The research, the exposure...it's the only way I'll become what I want to be.'

Her tone wasn't boastful. Just firm. Clear.

Pushkar nodded, absorbing it.

'I've never imagined a future that didn't involve medicine,' she continued. 'It's not a stepping stone. It's the whole path.'

Pushkar was quiet, moved in a way he hadn't expected. There was something about the clarity of her conviction—no theatrics, no self-pity—that left him humbled.

'You must really miss her,' he said finally.

'Every day,' she replied. 'But now I carry her with me. In every diagnosis, every paper I write, every night shift.'

He didn't know what to say. So he reached across the table and touched her hand. She didn't pull away.

⁓

The next morning, before the sky had even begun to lighten, Pushkar stood outside Hetal's hotel room, knocking gently, hands tucked into his pockets. The hallway smelled faintly of sea breeze and disinfectant.

After a long pause, the door cracked open. Hetal peeked out, her hair tousled and eyes half-lidded. 'Are you a lark or a lunatic?' she mumbled, rubbing her eyes.

Pushkar grinned. 'Maybe both. But mostly excited. I want to show you something.'

She narrowed her eyes suspiciously. 'Does it involve coffee?'

'Eventually,' he promised.

Ten minutes later, she emerged—blue denim

shorts, pink tank top and a light scarf around her neck. Pushkar handed her a helmet with mock ceremony and led her to the scooter he'd rented.

The roads were still quiet. As they rode through winding lanes and past sleepy shacks, the only sounds were the breeze in their ears and the occasional bark of a street dog. She sat close behind him, the scent of her freshly washed hair reaching him every time the wind shifted.

He didn't speak. Neither did she. But the silence didn't feel awkward.

'Where are we going?' Hetal asked after a while.

'You'll see,' he replied, smiling.

After half an hour, they pulled up at Vagator Beach. The sand was pale and soft, stretching into calm, jade-coloured waters. The sun had just begun its ascent, casting orange flecks across the horizon.

Hetal stepped down from the scooter and froze for a moment, taking it all in. 'It's beautiful,' she whispered.

They walked down to the shore, barefoot, the cold sand clinging to their feet. There were only a few other people—mostly locals stretching or walking their dogs. The emptiness felt like a secret.

Sitting side by side, legs buried in the sand, they watched the waves crash and retreat with rhythmic serenity. Neither spoke. There was nothing urgent to say. The moment was full.

Then, as if conjured by fate, a tea hawker wandered by, carrying a battered flask and small clay cups.

'Adrak wali?' he asked.

'Yes, please,' Pushkar said before Hetal could even nod.

They clinked their warm cups gently, steam curling into the morning air.

She smiled at him, her fingers curled around the shikora. 'This is…kind of perfect.'

He returned the smile, holding her gaze for a second too long.

And in that quiet moment, with the sea murmuring in the background and the world still stretching itself awake, something unspoken passed between them.

～०

Goodbyes are always difficult—but inevitable.

Hetal had to leave for Ahmedabad, Pushkar for Indore. The connection they'd formed wasn't casual; it clung to them like sea salt on skin, impossible to shake. With heaviness in their hearts and promises to keep, they returned to the routines they once found fulfilling.

In the weeks that followed, they spoke constantly— calls, texts, video chats, stolen hours despite time zones. Slowly but certainly, they knew: this wasn't a phase. This was it.

Pushkar couldn't imagine life without Hetal. He changed his status from single to committed with an ease that startled even him. Hetal, who had once built walls around her heart after her mother's death, found in Pushkar something she hadn't expected. Safety. Softness.

With him, she had begun exploring her own tenderness again—something she thought she'd lost forever.

Pushkar, too, felt something shift. He wanted to propose. He had never felt more certain of a future with someone. But there was one thing he hadn't shared— the one belief that had ended all his past relationships. And he didn't know if Hetal would understand. The fear of losing her lingered at the edge of every call, every unsaid word.

They were living in different countries, separated by distance and time zones, their longing for each other rising like hot mercury—uncontained and urgent.

~

It was December, and who wouldn't want to spend a holly, Californian Christmas?

Hetal had always imagined her ideal Christmas: snow-dusted pine trees, soft jazz in the background, the clink of red wine glasses by a window aglow with fairy lights. But this year, she chose something entirely different.

Pushkar hadn't been able to get his visa cleared in time. Deadlines, approvals, the usual red tape. So Hetal booked a ticket instead. A long-haul flight, two layovers and four hours of sleep later, she was in Indore—suitcase in hand, exhaustion tucked under a wide grin.

He met her at the airport in a red shirt and Santa cap, holding up a badly handwritten cardboard sign that read: 'Hetal Claus.' She burst out laughing the moment she saw him.

The days that followed were a whirlwind. He took her to Lalbagh Palace, guiding her through halls of faded grandeur, chandeliers heavy with history and quiet ballrooms that echoed their footsteps. She wasn't much for antiques or imperial stories, but she loved the way Pushkar narrated everything—as if Indore itself had grown up with him.

Afterwards, he led her to Chhappan Dukaan, the city's legendary food stretch. They moved slowly, sampling everything: khopra patties, dal bafla, hotdogs from Johny's, syrupy Frooti shakes and kulfis on wooden sticks. Hetal, who usually preferred Mediterranean salads and clean eating, threw caution to the wind.

By the fourth stall, she clutched her stomach. 'Do I look like a balloon yet?'

Pushkar snorted. 'Even if you did, you'd be a very cute one.'

Later that evening, they drove into a quiet residential colony where identical bungalows stood in rows like sleepy sentinels. At the very end of the lane was a small, deserted park. Pushkar stopped the car.

'There's something else,' he said.

Hetal raised an eyebrow. 'Should I be worried?'

He popped the trunk open and pulled out two plastic cups and a bottle of Scotch. 'This,' he announced proudly, 'is how we do Christmas in Indore.'

She laughed. 'Sitting in a car, drinking from plastic cups?'

He poured her drink with mock elegance. 'Ma'am, would you prefer neat or with soda?'

As they clinked cups inside the car, the radio hummed with an old Lucky Ali tune. Pushkar reached for the dashboard, pulled out a small cake box and opened it with a flourish.

'Pineapple pastry,' he said. 'With exactly one cherry on top. Because no Christmas is complete without cake.'

He fed her the first bite. Then, off-key but committed, he began to sing: 'We wish you a merry Christmas...and a happy new year...'

Hetal laughed so hard she nearly spilt her drink. 'You're unbelievable.'

'I try,' he said with a wink.

And even though there was no snow, no fireplace and definitely no jazz, Hetal felt strangely at home.

The next day, after hours of shopping at Sarafa Bazaar—sparkling bangles, block-printed suits, street food too tempting to resist—Hetal collapsed onto a bench outside Lassi Wala, cheeks flushed from the winter sun and endless haggling.

Pushkar returned from the counter holding two glasses of chilled buttermilk, beads of condensation already trickling down their sides.

'Is this your idea of post-shopping recovery?' Hetal asked, fanning herself with a paper napkin.

He handed her a glass. 'Trust me, it's better than wine right now.'

They sat opposite each other on an iron bench, legs almost touching. The street bustled around them— vendors shouting, children laughing, scooters zigzagging past. But in that tiny moment, it felt like only the two of them existed.

Pushkar reached into his sling bag and pulled out a small velvet box.

Hetal blinked. 'Wait—what...?'

He opened it, revealing not a diamond ring but a delicate gold pendant—Radha and Krishna, intertwined in eternal dance. It shimmered softly in the light.

'I didn't know your ring size,' he said, nervous now. 'And I didn't want to get it wrong. But this...this feels right.'

Her eyes widened.

'I want to spend my life with you, Hetal,' he said. 'Will you marry me?'

There was a pause. Her breath caught—not out of hesitation, but surprise. She looked at him for a long moment, then leaned forward and hugged him tightly.

'Yes,' she whispered into his ear. 'Yes, I want that too.'

Pushkar felt his heart thud like a drum, his fingers trembling with joy. He stood to place the pendant around her neck, his hands unsteady.

But Hetal gently stopped him, fingers on his wrist.

'Wait,' she said softly. 'There's something I have to tell you first.'

His smile faded, confusion flickering across his face.

She held his gaze. 'You know I have dreams, Pushkar. Dreams I've carried long before we met. I'm going to complete my specialization in Oncology in California. It's going to take years. And afterwards, I'll need to practise there, gain real-world experience. That's my path.'

He nodded slowly.

'I want us to be together,' she continued, 'but I won't be coming back to India anytime soon. If we marry... I'd need you with me. There. In California. Could you see yourself building a life with me there?'

The air between them shifted. Pushkar sat back down.

He had imagined proposing under stars, not conditions. He had been the one planning to drop a bombshell—the no-kids clause—but now Hetal had offered one of her own. And hers wasn't theoretical. It was mapped out, funded, already in motion.

He didn't answer. A part of him wanted to say yes, wanted to leap into her world just like that. But another part—the grounded, cautious part—sat heavy in his chest.

The moment lingered between them.

༄

The days after the proposal passed in a kind of haze.

They didn't fight. There were no raised voices, no ultimatums. But something had shifted. Conversations became shorter. Video calls lost their easy rhythm. They still messaged, still shared small joys—what they cooked, funny memes, daily work struggles—but the undercurrent was unmistakable. Something unsaid was growing too large to ignore.

Pushkar tried to convince himself that things would fall into place. That love was enough. But late at night, staring at the ceiling fan in his Indore apartment, doubts crept in like shadows.

He knew what he wanted. His roots were here—in the tea-scented back rooms of his family shop, in the streets of Indore that he knew like his own thoughts. He had plans, a business to grow, a legacy to revive. Moving to California didn't just mean shifting to Hetal's country; it meant abandoning his own.

And yet he missed her. He missed her voice, her questions, the way she rolled her eyes when she found him being overly philosophical. But he didn't say it. Pride tucked his feelings deep where no one could see.

Eventually, Hetal stopped pushing. She could hear it in his voice—the hesitation, the heaviness. And in her heart, she already knew.

They never officially broke up. There was no goodbye. Just a slow retreat into silence. Love doesn't always shatter. Sometimes it just...fades.

She buried herself in work—overnight shifts, patient charts, exam prep. It was easier to fill the hours than to sit with the ache of being left behind without being told.

But some wounds know how to whisper.

Every time she walked past a chai cart outside the hospital, the steam curling up into the California cold, she remembered him. The boy with the warm laugh and the Radha-Krishna pendant. The boy who had asked her to build a life, and then quietly stepped away from it.

Hetal told herself she understood. That he needed time. That love sometimes falters under pressure.

But some nights, when the world slowed down and no one needed saving, she'd find herself wondering: Was I too much? Or just not enough to make him stay?

༄

Months passed.

Pushkar launched himself into the family business. Long hours, market research, export strategies. From the outside, he looked like a man on the rise. Shah Teas began shipping overseas. He made it to the 'Forty Under Forty' shortlist. Friends congratulated him. His parents beamed. But inside, he was unravelling.

He stopped dressing up. Started skipping meals. His weight dropped. He snapped easily, cried alone, drifted through days in a fog of exhaustion. Everyone around him chalked it up to overwork. But his mother saw something else. She saw the boy who once wrote poems in a diary now avoiding mirrors.

She convinced him—gently, persistently—to see the family doctor. The diagnosis came like a quiet blow.

Early signs of depression.

'No meds yet,' the doctor said. 'But he needs help. Real help.'

Pushkar refused at first. 'I'm fine,' he snapped. 'I just need to sleep more.'

But sleep didn't come. Appetite didn't return. And eventually, silence became unbearable even to him.

His first few therapy sessions were a disaster. He barely spoke. Sat with his arms folded, eyes on the floor.

But the counsellor didn't push. She waited.

By the fourth session, he broke.

Not dramatically. Not with tears. But with a single sentence: 'I miss her.'

And once it started, it didn't stop. The hurt, the pride, the guilt, the confusion—he poured it all out. How he'd loved her. How he'd wanted to be strong. How he feared compromising would make him weak. How he'd let his fear dress itself as practicality.

The counsellor didn't offer advice. Just space. And slowly, in that space, Pushkar began to see something he hadn't before.

Love wasn't about giving in. It was about choosing again and again. And maybe choosing her didn't mean losing himself. Maybe it meant becoming more than what he was.

He sat with the realization for days. Not because he was unsure—but because he was scared.

What if she had moved on? What if the silence had hardened into something irreversible? The voice in his head—the same one that had once told him not to bend, not to yield—now whispered something softer: Go anyway.

He opened her chat thread more than once. Typed. Deleted. Typed again. Deleted again.

One evening, after another long session, Pushkar left the counselling centre with a clarity he hadn't felt in months.

He didn't rush home. He didn't draft a dramatic message or scroll through old photos. He simply sat on a bench outside and let the December wind thread through his hair.

He had spent so long protecting his version of independence that he hadn't realized what it had cost him. He had wanted to be strong. To seem decisive. But love wasn't weakness. It wasn't surrender. It was choosing someone—even when it meant changing course.

Later that night, he called Hetal. She was in class, but replied with a short message: 'Will call in 30?'

He didn't wait. He sent her a voice note instead. No rehearsals, no filters.

'Hetal... I was wrong. I kept thinking that compromising made me less of who I am. But I didn't see that loving you made me more. If the price of having you is California, then I'll pay it gladly. Because my life's not in a place—it's in the person I want to come home to. And that person is you.'

The message ended with a shaky breath.

She called back within five minutes.

And just like that, their orbit realigned.

They married a few months later in a small ceremony in Ahmedabad—no grand fanfare, just families, friends and a garland exchange under marigold lights. A week later, Pushkar boarded a flight to California with his wife, the Radha-Krishna pendant shining round her neck.

༄

Starting over was harder than he'd expected.

He missed home fiercely—missed roadside chai, his

mother's voice echoing through the kitchen, the way Indore lit up during festivals. But he built slowly. Step by step. He took Shah Teas online, opened dialogues with Indian grocery chains in the US and eventually carved out an export network that brought his family legacy across oceans.

Hetal was often exhausted—night duties, intense rotations, back-to-back exams. Their days together were brief but sacred. She'd come home, drop her bag by the door and collapse on to the couch. He'd bring her tea and rub her shoulders in silence. Some nights they didn't speak at all, just curled up under a shared blanket, watching mindless sitcoms and falling asleep mid-episode.

They weren't perfect. But they were together.

And five years later, they returned.

Goa hadn't changed much.

The palm trees still swayed with theatrical grace, the sea still shimmered like glass at midday, and Rock Café still played its old playlist, refusing to modernize. But Pushkar had changed. This time, as he sipped his margarita from a high stool overlooking the pool, it wasn't loneliness that sat beside him—it was memory.

The pool buzzed with noise. Children squealed as they splashed into the shallow end, calling out to parents in a chorus of 'Mumma! Papa!' A little boy clung to his father's neck while another wore oversized floaties and screamed with delight at every wave.

Pushkar watched it all quietly, a soft smile on his

lips. Once, the same sounds had annoyed him—too loud, too messy, too much. But now, something had shifted. He could see the joy on the parents' faces, how their eyes lit up at their kids' small victories in the water.

He hadn't thought about children in years—not seriously. But somewhere along the way—between long nights in California, Hetal's laughter echoing off their tiny apartment walls and the silent intimacy of lives slowly built—his resistance had softened.

He didn't see children as noise anymore. He saw them as possibility. Not a duty. Not a surrender. Just another way of loving fully. Of building something neither lonely nor legendary—but lasting. A new kind of adventure.

A woman in an orange swimsuit walked into the bar. She wore a loose wraparound, and sunglasses sat perched on her head. She slid on to the stool beside him without a word.

He turned, a knowing smile creeping across his face.

'Still staring at women in swimsuits, I see,' Hetal said, smirking.

He chuckled. 'Only one.'

She raised a brow. 'And?'

Pushkar took a deep breath, then leaned slightly closer. 'Would you mind making babies with me...and making this life even more complete?'

For a second, she just looked at him—caught somewhere between shock and amusement. Then she smiled. 'Only if it doesn't come with any terms and conditions,' she teased.

They both laughed, heads tipping toward each other in a moment that needed no ceremony.

He hadn't compromised. He had found love.

12

The Long Flight

Vimal could see Divya from afar, packing her bags and smiling to herself. They were finally going to Switzerland after years of planning. She had never taken such a long flight and was both excited and nervous. She had been to Switzerland over a thousand times in her dreams, but never had she thought it would truly happen.

Divya took out her blue chiffon sari and gazed at it. This sari always reminded her of Sridevi dancing in the ice-cold Alps to 'Tere Mere Hothon Pe'—the deep blue against white snow, the impossible glamour of it all. She used to wonder how the actresses didn't freeze in such scanty clothing. She folded it gently and placed it in the suitcase. She had decided—she would wear it at Titlis, no matter what.

This trip had stirred something long buried. As she sat before the mirror that evening, the overhead light caught every line she had once ignored. Fine wrinkles creased her forehead, and the once-tight skin around her eyes had softened. The freckles across her cheeks had darkened with time. Her body had borne more than age—it had carried pain, secrets, surgery scars and silence.

Her eyelashes were still thick, but they no longer framed a girl. They framed a woman who had lived decades of devotion, disappointment and duty. She was nearing fifty now. So many years had passed in caring for others that she hadn't noticed herself fading at the edges.

She had aged. Not unpleasantly—but unnoticed. She picked up her phone and booked a facial appointment right away. She wanted to look beautiful for Switzerland. Or maybe...for him.

Vimal reminded her to pack medicines. He told her, gently but firmly, not to carry her snacks ka pitara this time—but she still tucked in his favourite theplas, achar and bhujia. Just in case.

By 4 a.m. the next morning, Divya was up, too excited to stay in bed longer. Vimal kept snoozing alarms till six, but eventually they made it out. By the time they left, she had watered all the plants, locked every door and window, and instructed the gardener and house staff carefully. The house would rest while she finally lived her dream.

It was her first international journey. Vimal had

travelled abroad several times for work, but this was different. As the flight took off, he noticed her glow. She looked childlike, scrolling through the in-flight movies with wonder. When the air hostess asked about beverages, she chose white wine. Day drinking wasn't her habit, but that day felt worth the exception.

Divya crossed her legs and sat upright. She closed her eyes and played her meditation track through her ear pods. Shishir Sadhana was a practice she never skipped, not even in transit. Meditation had been her shield through seasons of storm, a ritual that steadied her breath when the world spun too fast.

Vimal watched her quietly. There was something unspoken between them—warmth, yes, but something heavier too. He had tried, over the past few months, to talk to her. Tried to broach things delicately, to begin a conversation. But each time, she had sensed it—his pauses, his hesitations—and slipped away. Into another room. Off to her mother's. Behind the curtain of politeness.

Now, sitting next to her 35,000 feet above the ground, he realized this might be his only moment. He wasn't proud of what he was about to do. But he also knew there was no easy way.

He reached into his bag and pulled out a folder. His hands trembled slightly. For a moment, he considered putting it back inside. Maybe it could wait till after landing. But the plane felt like the only place left where she couldn't walk away—where silence couldn't save them both.

He placed the folder gently on the tray table in front of her.

Divya opened her eyes and stretched. She noticed the folder and looked at Vimal, confused. He gave her a slight nod—more a plea than a gesture. Her smile faded. Her hand hovered over the papers. Something inside her knew.

The moment she saw the first page, her chest tightened. Her ears filled with a muffled hum, her vision blurred. She tried to blink, to breathe, but her fingers were shaking.

Her voice cracked as she whispered, 'Why now? Why here?'

Vimal looked down. 'I tried, Divya,' he said softly. 'I tried for months to talk to you about this. But every time I even hinted, you shut it down. You'd change the topic. Stand up mid-sentence. Walk away. I didn't know how else to reach you.'

'You're blaming me for this?'

'I'm not blaming you,' he said gently. 'I'm saying we both stopped speaking.'

She looked away, biting back tears.

His voice broke a little. 'I didn't bring you here to hurt you. I brought you here because I owed you this— your dream. You deserve it. But I couldn't put this off anymore. Not because I wanted to ruin this moment. But because I didn't know when I'd get another one where we could just...talk.'

Divya stared at him, her heart pounding. 'Talk? Is this what you call talking?'

Vimal's shoulders slumped. 'I'm not proud of this. I don't think I ever imagined it would come to this. But I've been carrying it around for so long. Watching your joy only made it worse. I know what this place means to you. That's why I waited till you had it.'

He finally looked at her—his eyes full of weariness, not anger. 'I wanted you to see the mountains. To breathe here. Even if I'm no longer part of the picture you carry home.'

Divya couldn't believe her ears. Had Vimal become so heartless that he had chosen to turn the place of her best dream into the place of her worst nightmare? She felt betrayed, broken, fragile and vulnerable.

'You waited thirty years to do this? Why now?'

Vimal closed his eyes. 'My mother's dying, Divya. She's barely holding on. And the only thing she keeps asking for—every day, every night—is to see the face of her grandson before she goes.' His voice trembled. 'You know how she is. You know what family means to her. To all of us.'

Divya sat silently, her throat dry.

'I tried to forget that dream,' he continued. 'Tried to accept that we had a daughter and that was it. But it never went away. Not for me. Not for her. It just slept inside me.'

He swallowed hard. 'And then the doctors said she may not last the year. That's when it all came rushing back. The weight of her disappointment. The rituals left undone. The silence in the family tree. I know how it sounds, Divya—I do. But in my world, having a son isn't just desire. It's duty.'

Divya stared at him. 'So you're leaving me to chase a ghost.'

'I'm trying to give my mother peace. Before she goes. I know what I'm doing is wrong. I know I'm wrong. I know this is cruel. But I feel like I'm drowning in expectations—hers, the family's, the world's. And yours…'

'My expectations?' she asked quietly.

'That you'd keep holding on. That I could keep disappointing you and you'd never break. You never did. You just…endured.'

She said nothing.

'You weren't running from me, Divya. You were running from the truth. Because you thought if you didn't hear it, it wouldn't become real.'

She turned her face away, blinking fast.

He continued, gently, 'You were always the stronger one. Holding everything together. This house, the family, your own pain. I don't blame you for protecting what was left. But we've been living inside a silence for too long.'

She swallowed hard. 'I thought…if I didn't say it, if I didn't name it, we could still be something. You might come back to me.'

'I never truly left,' he said again. 'But I haven't been present for a long time either.'

Vimal had stayed married to Divya not because he wanted to, but because he couldn't leave. He worked under Divya's father, a man of considerable influence and rigid values. Though he had never stood up for her, never offered shelter, his silent presence had been enough to keep Vimal from crossing certain lines. He hadn't blessed their union—but he hadn't allowed its dissolution either.

Divya had given all that she had to be the mother of a son. She conceived several times. Each time, the process was the same—bribed doctors, quiet tests, swift endings. She carried those absences in her body, and they hollowed her. Her nights were sleepless, her appetite vanished. Eventually, her body gave up. The doctors said she could no longer conceive. Outwardly, she mourned. Inwardly, she gave thanks—she didn't want to be a murderer anymore.

After that, Vimal gave up. His hope faded, and so did his affection. He had once doted on Aadhya, but that faded too. Slowly, she became not a blessing but the misstep that had denied him a son. He wanted her married early, gone before she could ask for more.

But Aadhya had inherited her mother's quiet steel. She refused to shrink. She wanted to study, to fly, to choose. Her rebellion shook the house. Vimal snapped. He severed ties. Divya was forbidden to call or speak of her again.

But Divya found her way. Through her father, she got brief, careful updates. Aadhya was studying again. She was flying. She was rising.

And Aadhya knew.

Her grandfather, distant and unsentimental, had told her the truth: what her mother had endured. He hadn't defended Divya in her marriage—but he made sure her daughter saw her strength.

Divya never heard Aadhya's voice. But she carried each whisper like a prayer.

A soft chime rang through the cabin.

'Today we have special guests on board,' came the announcement. 'And we request them to please stand as we welcome and applaud them. Mr Vimal and Mrs Divya Rathore—parents of our most talented and successful pilot, Miss Aadhya Rathore. May her story inspire every Indian girl to chase their dreams and make the country proud.'

Divya froze. Vimal stared in disbelief.

And then the cockpit door opened.

Aadhya stepped out, tall and composed in her pilot's uniform. Her face calm, her eyes unwavering. She walked down the aisle with quiet grace, stopped in front of them and bent to touch Divya's feet.

Divya could barely breathe. Her hands trembled as she placed them on her daughter's head.

Her heart had found its home again.

Aadhya rose, her eyes meeting her mother's. No words passed between them, but something shifted. Something returned.

Divya turned to Vimal, her voice steady, clear. 'I am thankful to you—for this long flight.'

And then, without hesitation, she signed the divorce papers.

13

Knowledge Is Power

The clucking of my two little creatures calms me—it's the sound of satisfaction, of belonging. I smile, watching them nibble away at carrots, watercress, spinach and bok choy. These are luxuries I never tasted growing up. Back then, I fed them coriander stems and wilted greens from other people's backyards.

These two white rabbits are not just pets. They are a reminder of where I come from—and perhaps, how far I've come.

I remember the day they entered my life. It was during my days as a junior party worker, serving under my mentor, MLA Aurobindo-da. Our party was small, always in financial distress, and our 'office' was barely more than a dingy box with no windows and peeling paint. Old comrades sat around a stone slab playing carrom, trading tales of past glories between strikes.

I preferred holding meetings in the park—on patches of fake grass, away from the mosquitoes and gloom. Sunshine, I believed, brought not just light but a sense of hope.

That afternoon, while I was in the middle of assigning roles and mapping outreach strategies, my comrades interrupted me with a sudden outburst of song: 'Happy birthday to you...' they sang, with full throats and clapping hands. Jayanto shook a bottle of Thums Up like champagne, and Neera handed out chicken rolls and biryani boxes.

I was stunned. I hadn't celebrated my birthday in years—not since my mother would cook prawn curry, light up our lane with borrowed bulbs from a local shop and let us play cricket under the stars.

Just when I thought the celebration was over, Jayanto stepped forward with a heavy steel box covered in pink cotton cloth.

'The best is saved for the last, sir. Kindly open this small gift from all of us.'

'Small? It looks like a trunk!' I laughed, unwrapping it.

Inside, a silver cage held two tiny white rabbits. I was caught between surprise and confusion—was this a joke, or an actual gift? I forced a smile.

'You like it, sir?' Aparna asked, eyes gleaming.

'Very much,' I replied, not entirely convincingly.

That day, I didn't understand what they meant by giving me living creatures as a gift. But over the years, I've come to realize—they weren't just pets. They were companions. Silent witnesses to a life that had barely begun to bloom.

These two rabbits saw everything. They saw me climb from foot soldier to leader. They saw the compromises, the quiet heartbreaks, the relentless ascent. And perhaps, even now, they understand more than they let on.

After folding the newspaper and sipping my morning tea, I called out to check if my children were ready. Today was different. I had been invited to inaugurate a school—my first such invitation—and for once, the committee had insisted I bring my children.

Normally Lopa and Somu skip these events. They find them tedious, too full of people calling me 'sir' and asking for photos. This time, their mother persuaded them. Lopa only agreed on the condition that I would call her Lops, and Somnath, Sam, in public.

'Why do they want to twist such beautiful names?' I muttered to myself, slightly annoyed.

As we approached the school, the building rose before us like a palace: sleek glass, sweeping lawns, even a space for horse riding. Inside, there was a computer lab, an aviation wing with simulators and a modern library that could rival a university.

They ushered us in with garlands, cameras flashing, voices cheering. For a moment, I stood tall. My children saw how others looked at me—not as their old-fashioned father but as a man who mattered. I thought they'd be proud.

The principal spoke eloquently. Then it was my turn. I took the mic and shared what I always do: the importance of education, and the sacred role of parents and teachers in nurturing young minds.

That's when a voice from the media corner pierced the moment. 'Sir, may I ask about your own education?'

It felt like someone had knocked the air from my lungs. I wasn't ashamed—but I was unprepared. I looked instinctively towards my children. Instead of reassurance, I saw something else. Uncertainty? Embarrassment? My son looked away. My daughter's jaw tightened.

I steadied myself. I could have answered truthfully— about how I studied through life, not school. But instead, I smiled and said, 'Today, I'd rather not shift the spotlight on to myself. This moment belongs to the school. May it continue to nurture and empower the minds of tomorrow.'

The audience clapped. The cameras moved on. But as I descended the stage, the echo of my children's expressions clung to me.

Had I failed them by never finishing school? Or had I failed them by never showing them what that sacrifice meant?

By the time we returned home, my legs ached with the weight of the day. The car ride had been mostly quiet—my children stared out their windows, earbuds in, lost in a world I didn't understand.

The house was unusually quiet. The staff had taken the day off and Nilanjana was napping, a thin blanket rising and falling with her gentle breath. I watched her for a moment—so still, so unburdened—and couldn't bring myself to wake her.

I shuffled into the kitchen, disoriented. The steel tins, the jars of spices, the drawers—it had been years since I had cooked anything with my own hands. *I used to be good at this*, I thought. Once, every meal had come from my hands.

I was still trying to find the chai-patti when I heard footsteps.

'Lost, Baba?' Somnath grinned, stepping inside.

I nodded sheepishly.

'Move over. I've got this,' he said, gently nudging me aside.

I stood awkwardly, watching as he boiled water, measured the red tea leaves, added a touch of sugar. Then he reached into a cabinet for murmura and mustard oil, chopped some green chillies and onions, and sliced a lemon.

'What's all that for?' I asked.

'Jhalmuri,' he said casually. 'Maa's told us a dozen times how much you love it. Especially the ones you bought near Victoria, back in the day. She says you'd hold her hand, sing to her and eat it straight from the paper cone.'

I blinked, taken aback. 'She remembers all that?'

'Of course she does. She says it was her happiest time.'

I felt my throat tighten.

'How did you learn to cook like this?' I asked.

He shrugged. 'From Maa. And for Maa. She gets so excited when I cook—even if it's just toast. She says it reminds her that we care.'

I watched his hands move—the way he squeezed the lemon, sprinkled the salt. He looked so much older in that moment. Not the boy I remembered dropping off for his first day of school.

'You never told me you knew how to cook,' I said softly.

'You never asked,' he replied, not unkindly.

He handed me a steel glass of tea and a small plate of jhalmuri.

'Taste test?'

I sipped. Then took a bite. The flavours hit like a memory—sharp, warm, utterly familiar.

A tear fell before I could stop it. 'It's...perfect,' I said.

'Good,' he replied, a little too fast. Then, after a pause, his expression shifted. A small line formed between his brows. 'Baba?'

'Yes?'

'Why didn't you say anything at the school today? When that reporter asked about your education?'

I sighed, letting the question hang. The warmth from the cup seeped into my palms, but it couldn't thaw the chill I suddenly felt in my chest.

'Because I didn't know how to answer it in that moment,' I admitted. 'Not without turning it into something about me. And today wasn't supposed to be about me.'

'It felt wrong,' Somu said queitly. 'Like they tried to make you feel less. And you let them.'

I looked at him, unsure how to explain the decades of silence I'd swallowed.

'Do you think…do you think I should have answered?' I asked.

He paused, then said, 'We felt awkward…not because you're uneducated, Baba—but because the world still thinks that matters most. That a paper certificate defines someone's worth.'

I looked away. 'Maybe I felt that too, for a second. That twinge of doubt.'

'But you shouldn't,' he said. 'You taught yourself everything. Maa always says you never stopped learning. That you have read more than most professors. That you listen, you question, you absorb things like a sponge. I've seen it.'

His words touched something raw. I nodded slowly, unsure whether to smile or cry again.

The tea had gone cold in my hands, but inside, something warm had returned.

When Nilanjana and I got married, I was still a small-time party worker—full of slogans and ideals, proud to be leading the youth wing under Aurobindo-da's watchful eyes. We barely had enough for rent, but I thought I had the world figured out.

After Aurobindo-da passed away, everything unravelled. The old guard clung to their habits, the young wanted revolution. Meetings turned into arguments, plans dissolved into delays. The party lacked a leader—and the fractures widened.

I didn't plan to fill that space. I just kept showing up. I organized rallies, listened to grievances, cleaned up local ponds with my own hands when the municipal board failed to act. Slowly, people started looking to me—not because I was loud, but because I understood what they needed.

I never hid where I came from. I wore my old slippers and cotton kurta long after I could afford better. I spoke in Bengali when others switched to English. I wasn't polished, but I was real.

The public responded. And the party noticed.

Of course, not everyone was pleased. The senior members disliked my 'aggressive' methods. They called it disruptive. I called it necessary.

'He's too emotional,' some said.

'He's too ambitious,' others whispered.

They were right, maybe. But I never wanted to rise alone—I pulled others up with me. I created local reading centres, started night schools, supported first-time candidates. My strength was never in strategy—it was in people.

Somewhere along the way, I stopped being the foot soldier. I became the face. MLA. Then MP.

And through it all—every late-night campaign, every missed anniversary, every Sunday spent in committee meetings instead of at the zoo with the twins—Nilanjana stood by me.

I wasn't even there when our children were born. I was leading a padyatra through flood-hit villages. When I finally reached the hospital, Somnath and Lopa were already swaddled in her arms. She didn't complain. She just smiled and asked if I'd eaten.

'They have your eyes,' she'd whispered.

For years, she raised them without me. She attended every parent-teacher meeting, every doctor's visit, every school play. She learnt how to do everything I couldn't.

Sometimes, I wonder if they even need me.

But tonight, watching Somu stir jhalmuri for me, quoting things his mother told him—tonight, I realized she hadn't raised them alone.

She raised them with my stories.

I stared at him, his words hanging in the space between us like light through steam. 'You really believe that?'

A new voice cut in.

'I do.'

Lopa stood leaning against the doorframe, arms crossed, smiling faintly.

'You're my role model, Baba. Always have been.'

I swallowed hard.

I stared at them, then said softly, 'You know... I wanted to study. When I was little, the government had just started free schooling. I used to stand outside the gates, watching children walk in with slates and books and dreams I didn't yet have words for. But after your grandfather lost his thumb in a factory accident, there was no choice. We needed money. Someone had to step up. That someone was me.'

'Did he ask you to?' asked Lopa

'Never. He just said, "Come with me tomorrow. I'll show you how the welding works." That was all.' I smiled faintly. 'He taught me everything with one good hand. How to mend wires. How to listen to machines like they were speaking. Every broken part was a puzzle, every repair a lesson.'

I paused. 'And he blamed himself, I think. Quietly. Always. But he made sure I never stopped learning.'

They didn't speak, so I continued.

'Your grandmother—your maa's namesake—was no less a teacher. She brought home torn newspapers, comics, outdated textbooks from the kabadiwala. She'd lay them out like sacred texts. We'd read *Panchatantra* stories in Bengali, then she'd ask what I learnt from them. She'd tear editorials from the front page and say, "Explain this to me like you are a schoolteacher." She'd never been to school herself, but she had the fire of ten scholars.'

'That's why we love reading too,' Lopa said quietly. 'It's in us.'

'She sounds incredible,' Somu whispered.

'She was. She taught me that learning has nothing to do with walls or blackboards. "Ask the fish seller. Ask the bank clerk. Ask the sweeper. Knowledge wears no badge," she'd say.'

I looked at both of them—my children, so different and yet somehow carrying pieces of all that came before them.

'Still,' I admitted, 'there's a moment—every time someone asks me about degrees—where something inside me goes blank. Like I'm not enough.'

Lopa stepped forward. 'You are more than enough, Baba.'

I closed my eyes for a moment, letting their words sink in.

'You know,' I said, voice lighter now, 'someone once asked me where I studied. I told him I graduated from the University of...Thirst for Knowledge.'

They both laughed.

'That sounds made-up,' Somnath grinned.

'It is,' I said, smiling. 'But it's true, all the same.'

I lowered myself into my old rocking chair, the wooden arms warm from the afternoon light. Outside, I could hear the faint rustle of the rabbits in their pen.

The journalist's question still echoed in my head— but it didn't sting anymore.

For the first time, I felt the answer—not as defence, but as truth. I had never stopped learning. And I had never stopped teaching.

That, I finally understood, was the only qualification I ever needed.

14

Eyes Wouldn't Fool Anymore

She stretched her hands and, with some effort, brought the harmonium down from the loft. After carefully placing it on the floor, she dusted it gently with a piece of satin cloth. It was a special day. She was expecting someone—her new harmonium teacher.

Priyamvada was a trained singer, but learning to play an instrument was something new. Singing made her happy, but after marriage and motherhood, riyaaz had slowly faded from her life. She wouldn't have thought to return to it on her own, but Sunil—observant as always—noticed.

One day, he said quietly, 'You should start singing again.' She smiled, brushing it off, but he pressed on. 'Why not call a teacher? It'll bring structure…and maybe you could learn to play too.'

She poured lukewarm water into a glass, added rock salt and gargled, preparing her throat. As soon as she heard footsteps, she rushed to the door to open it, then paused, taken aback.

She had never seen eyes quite that shade of blue. Mihir was tall, fair, with a quiet presence. His black hair, drenched from the rain, clung to his forehead. She invited him in. He entered with a polite smile, his manner earnest but easy.

After a brief introduction, Mihir helped her carry the harmonium to the balcony that opened towards the portico. They sat on a patterned rug, side by side, facing the flowerbed. Rain still dripped rhythmically from the sloping roof. The world around them had gone hush— as if waiting for music.

Mihir positioned the instrument, adjusted its bellows, and nodded.

'Let's begin,' he said. 'You sing. I'll follow.'

She started gently, unsure, but soon her tone gained clarity. Her voice—euphonious, layered, almost haunting—filled the air. Mihir followed on the harmonium, shifting keys in tune with her notes. Her eyes were closed. She was lost in the music.

When Priya stopped, there was a pause—as if even the breeze had been listening.

'You have a strong grasp,' Mihir said, after a moment. 'But the voice needs polishing. More riyaaz, before we get to the keys. You're not a beginner, Priya ji—just a little out of practice.'

After Mihir left, Priya sat still for a few minutes. A

strange warmth bloomed inside her—part memory, part melody. She hadn't felt this light in years.

She laughed suddenly, pinched her arm, and whispered to herself, 'Bravo!'

Then she jumped up and hurried to the kitchen. She wanted to cook something special for the evening.

When Sonu returned from school and Sunil from office, they were greeted not just by the scent of moong dal pakodi and mint chutney, but by something else—a change in the air. A liveliness. Priya helped Sonu change, handed Sunil his towel and pyjamas, and returned to the kitchen humming.

'La la laa laa...' she sang softly, spreading the pakoras on to the plate, with mint chutney on the side. Her movements had a rhythm, a lightness that made the entire space feel warmer.

As they sat down to eat, Sunil's eyes rested on Priya's face. She was smiling, genuinely, and it lit up the room in a way he hadn't seen for a long while.

While sipping her cardamom tea, Priya began speaking—animated, eager, as if the words had been waiting inside her for years.

She told him everything—how Mihir appreciated her voice, how he guided her through the notes, how much more she needed to practise. She laughed mid-sentence, caught herself, then kept going. Her voice didn't stop, and neither did her hands. She served, poured, adjusted Sonu's cushion, all while narrating her rediscovery of music.

Sunil listened quietly, watching her, letting her words

fill the silences that had once made up their evenings.

It felt like a breeze had swept through their home, lifting something heavy off the floorboards.

Priya had something to look forward to again. And he, too, felt something stir—a pride, a cautious joy—as he watched his wife return to herself.

Priya practised every morning without fail. Once Sunil and Sonu left, she would glide through her chores with surprising ease—as if time had loosened its grip. By mid-morning, she'd settle in front of the harmonium. Her voice, once tentative, had started to stretch and strengthen, like a limb remembering how to move.

The house filled with music. Not from a speaker, but from somewhere real—somewhere within her.

Sunil noticed. She smiled more. She walked differently. The house felt warmer. Even his mother, on a Sunday call, remarked, 'She's glowing these days, beta. You did the right thing—not many men push their wives to follow old dreams.'

Sunil felt a quiet pride, but alongside it came something else—a dull hum in the background. He couldn't name it.

At dinner, Priya spoke with excitement about *alap* and *taan*, breath control, voice texture, new *bandish*es. She spoke like someone discovering language again.

Sunil listened with interest. But sometimes, as she described a tricky shift in scale or the way Mihir had shown her a hidden note in a raga, his thoughts slipped. *What place do I hold in this new rhythm of hers?*

It wasn't jealousy. Not exactly. Just a subtle sense of

standing on the periphery of something once shared.

One afternoon, Sunil returned from office earlier than usual. The living room was quiet. On the balcony, Priya sat facing the garden, speaking softly into her phone.

'No no, Mihir sir, you've already done enough. I'll practise this one on my own today,' she said, her voice calm. Then, after a pause: 'I know... I'm lucky.'

Sunil didn't move. He stood by the door, letting the words settle.

Then he stepped in, louder than needed, letting the sound of his bag hitting the table announce him.

Priya turned. 'You're early! Hungry?' she said brightly.

He smiled. 'Starving.'

That week, Mihir arrived for their lesson looking more serious than usual.

'There's something I wanted to tell you,' he said, settling beside the harmonium. 'There's a singing competition happening here in Nashik—in twelve weeks.'

Priya looked up sharply. 'A competition?'

He nodded. 'A big one. State level. I think you should participate.'

Her mouth opened, then closed again. 'That...that has always been a dream,' she said. 'But I'm not ready.'

Mihir didn't relent. 'Not yet. But you can be. If you push.'

She hesitated. 'Will you come more often? Maybe every other day?'

Mihir shook his head. 'I can't. I'm in the middle of hospital rotations. My internship is getting more intensive.'

She looked disappointed. He read it immediately.

He paused, then added, 'It's not about unwillingness. Just exhaustion. Teaching you already takes the best of my free hours. But...'

He saw something in her expression. Something childlike. Something that still believed.

'I'll try,' he said. 'Evenings. After hospital. If we both stay committed.'

Priya lit up. 'Yes. I will. I promise.'

And so they began. The lessons became more regular. Their conversations drifted from scales and *sur* to childhoods, first performances, old heartbreaks, odd habits. They joked. Teased. Learnt each other's patterns.

'You look exhausted,' Priya said one evening as he slumped over the harmonium.

'It was a rough shift. Some patients just stay with you,' he said, running a hand through his hair. 'It's not just physical. It's emotional.'

Without a word, she slipped into the kitchen and returned with ginger tea. He accepted it gratefully, their fingers brushing.

As he played, he looked lost again—not in music this time, but in thought. Priya watched him quietly. She had come to understand this part of him—how deeply he felt, how quickly he connected.

Sometimes she teased him, 'Aise toh tum doctor ban gaye, singer hi theek hai tumhare liye—you may have become a doctor, but being a singer suits you better.'

He'd laugh, a tired but real laugh.

Then one evening, the skies darkened suddenly. Rain

came pouring down, hard and heavy. The breeze turned cool and sharp.

Mihir was still seated at the harmonium, eyes distant.

Without thinking, Priya took his hand. 'Come. We're going out.'

He resisted. 'Are you mad, Priya ji? We'll fall sick.'

'Don't be such a bore, sir,' she grinned, already dragging him towards the garden. 'This rain has come to recharge us. How can we not greet it?'

She began singing, spinning, drenched. Mihir watched for a moment—then joined her, laughing, his voice rising in harmony. He picked a wild jasmine from a bush and tucked it behind her ear.

The white flower glowed in her dark curls like a moon caught in a cloud.

As they stepped back inside, drenched and breathless, Priya laughed—not loudly, but deeply, like someone who had been holding her breath for too long. Mihir watched her, something soft flickering behind his tired eyes.

Then a pause. A tightening in the air.

He turned quickly to the harmonium, wiping its keys dry with a corner of his sleeve. The laughter faded into a silence neither of them knew how to name.

'You know,' he said, not looking up, 'you sing better when your heart is light.'

Priya smiled, catching his mood. 'Then keep lightening it.'

Mihir hesitated. 'People might...misread what they see.'

She looked at him steadily. 'Then let them listen instead.'

He chuckled softly. 'You remind me why I love this art. But let's keep it that—art. Music. Nothing more.'

She nodded.

After she changed into dry clothes, she brought two cups of hot water laced with honey and sat back beside him. The moment in the rain lingered in the air between them, unspoken. But it didn't hang heavy. Not yet.

The next day, Priya sat watching an episode of *Indian Idol*. A contestant was speaking about choosing a song that 'lived inside their voice.' The phrase struck her like a sudden note—precise, unexpected.

What song lived inside her voice?

She stared at the harmonium. For the first time in weeks, it looked like a stranger.

She tried singing a few lines, but her voice faltered. Her fingers trembled as she reached for a glass of water. She sipped. Then the glass fell.

Panic settled into her bones.

Without thinking, she picked up her phone and dialled Mihir.

Mihir arrived quickly, worry written across his face. He didn't wait for a formal greeting—he simply saw her pale expression, and instinctively pulled her into a hug.

'Are you all right? What happened?' he asked, voice full of concern.

At that precise moment, Sunil stepped inside, office bag still slung over his shoulder. He froze.

Before him stood Mihir, arms around Priya. Her face turned towards him, flushed. Her body language, unsettled. Mihir's expression, unreadable.

A flicker crossed Sunil's face—not fury yet, but the sharp stab of disbelief. In that instant, memory flooded in: the neighbour's careless remark about dancing in the rain, the jasmine flower he had seen drying in a corner dish, Priya's distant laughter and the quiet closeness he had begun to feel edged out of.

'Priya?' he said, voice brittle.

Startled, she turned. 'Sunil—'

Then she rushed to him and wrapped her arms around his waist, sobbing into his shirt. Her tears weren't for guilt, but for the collapse of something she had worked to protect.

Sunil stood stiff. His gaze shifted to Mihir.

'What's going on?' he asked, though he was no longer really asking.

Mihir stepped back slightly, his voice even. 'She called me. She was panicking about the competition. I came to help.'

Sunil's jaw tightened. 'And you thought holding her was appropriate?'

Before Priya could respond, he pushed Mihir hard. Mihir stumbled, catching himself on the table edge.

'You pervert! I welcomed you into our home—trusted you—'

Mihir's face flushed. 'I respect you both.'

'Respect?' Sunil barked. 'Giving her flowers? Dancing in the rain? The whole neighbourhood saw you!'

Shaking with rage, Mihir stepped forward and grabbed Sunil's collar. 'You act like you support her—like you want her to have dreams. But the moment she starts living them, you can't stand it.'

'Don't lecture me,' Sunil snapped. 'You've been manipulating her.'

'Stop it!' Priya shouted, stepping between them. 'Enough. Both of you.'

Mihir looked at her then—really looked. Her face, terrified. Her voice, torn. Her presence, fraying between the two men. Something inside him stilled.

He let go. 'I didn't come here for this,' he said softly.

And without another word, he turned and walked out into the rain.

Priya collapsed onto the sofa. Her voice, when it came, was barely a whisper.

'Sunil...you broke something in me tonight.'

He looked at her, stunned.

'I always thought of you as a man of sense, of calm, of strength. But tonight, you let your eyes lie to you. And your ears fool you.'

Sunil opened his mouth, but she raised a hand.

'Mihir was here because I called him. I panicked. I didn't know what to do. And I needed support—from him, and from you. But you—you chose to doubt me. Not gently. Not even silently. But violently.'

He stood silent.

'And the rain?' she added bitterly. 'If a working woman laughs with a male colleague, it's nothing. If a housewife does the same, it's scandal? Why? Why is my joy suspect just because I sing it in the company of a man?'

She turned fully toward him now, her voice steadier. 'Mihir is my guru. My friend. He's engaged to a woman

I speak to regularly. She's proud of the friendship we've built. But you—you forgot that I am worthy of that kind of friendship.'

She stopped, breath catching, not because she was out of words—but because she no longer knew if he deserved more.

That night, Sunil lay awake long after the house had fallen silent.

The ceiling fan hummed above, but his thoughts were louder—looping images of Priya sobbing into his chest, Mihir's stunned expression, and the sharp clarity of her words: 'You broke something in me.'

He had thought he was protecting her. Protecting them. But now he saw it—it wasn't protection. It was fear disguised as love.

At dawn, he sat on the edge of the bed, watching Priya help Sonu with his shoelaces. She was calm, gentle, efficient. But her smile didn't reach her eyes.

She had withdrawn—not out of anger, but something colder. Disappointment.

In the days that followed, she continued her routine. She cooked, cleaned, helped Sonu with homework. But the music had vanished. No riyaaz. No humming. Not even casual notes under her breath.

Sunil noticed the quiet—and how it stretched between them like a wall. The house felt hollow, like a radio left on mute.

Mihir didn't call. Nor did Priya. The silence between them was mutual, respectful, and aching.

Mihir, on his side, sat in his room late at night,

replaying the confrontation over and over. Not the words. Not the push. But her—Priya—caught between two men, her voice breaking under weight it hadn't earned.

He spoke to Devyani that night.

'I didn't cross a line,' he said. 'But...maybe I was too present.'

Devyani was quiet for a while. Then she said, 'Sometimes lines don't have to be crossed to be threatened. But if something good was hurt by fear, we can still try to repair it.'

She booked a train to Nashik.

∽

A week passed, quiet and slow. Then one breezy morning Priya was in the garden plucking hibiscus for her morning puja, when she heard the main gate creak open. She looked up, shielding her eyes from the sun.

A young woman with warm eyes, honey-toned skin, and thick waves of shoulder-length hair came down the garden path. She wore a simple pink T-shirt that matched the bougainvillaea overhead.

'Hello, Priya. I'm Devyani.'

Priya blinked in surprise. Then instinctively smiled back. There was something sincere in the girl's face—open, unafraid. Without a word, she hugged her.

Inside, Sunil was at the dining table, reading headlines on his phone and waiting for tea.

Priya walked in with Devyani. 'This is Devyani,' she said gently. 'Mihir's fiancée.'

Sunil removed his glasses. 'Fiancée?'

Devyani smiled and nodded. 'I came straight from the station. Sorry to drop in like this. But I had to come.'

He nodded slowly, still processing.

Priya handed her a cup of tea. 'Black, no sugar.'

Devyani raised an eyebrow. 'How did you know?'

'Mihir told me,' Priya replied with a soft laugh. 'Along with how you weaned him off milk tea to stop his...digestive commentary.'

They both giggled. Sunil gave a small, confused smile, trying to catch up.

Then Devyani turned to him. 'Sunil ji, I know what happened last week. Mihir didn't tell me out of anger. He just...needed someone to understand.'

Sunil looked down.

'I'm not here to blame. I'm here because someone's dream is in danger. And someone else is quietly letting it slip through her fingers.'

She turned to Priya. 'You gave up music once. Now you're doing it again—for someone else's comfort.'

She looked back at Sunil. 'She spoke of you with such pride. That you encouraged her, gave her the nudge she needed. But trust, Sunil ji, is not built once. It's practised—like riyaaz.'

The room fell still.

'I'm not asking you to apologize to me. Or to Mihir. Just ask yourself—did you listen to her? Or did you only watch her?'

Sunil looked up. His throat was dry. He wanted to speak, to explain, but the words weren't there.

Priya looked torn, her eyes brimming. 'Devyani... you're kind, and I'm thankful, but Sunil is my husband. I can't let someone else tell him he was wrong. That's our bond to mend. Not yours to judge.'

Sunil looked at her, struck.

'It's not about permission. It's about rebuilding trust,' Priya added. 'And I can't do that by disobeying him. I want him to see that I chose him—even when I had a chance to walk away.'

She looked at Sunil now, her voice even.

'I spoke loudly that day. I stood up for myself. Every word I said—about friendship, about dignity—I meant. And I still do.'

She turned to Devyani again. 'I will sing. But only if he sits in the front row.'

Sunil blinked. His throat caught.

'I've already chosen you, Priya,' he said, voice unsteady. 'I just didn't know how to say it.'

He stepped forward.

'You believed in me even after I failed you. You gave up your dream so I wouldn't feel threatened. But it wasn't strength that stopped you. It was love. And I mistook it for guilt. I thought I was protecting us. But really, you were the one protecting me.'

His eyes welled, and this time, he didn't wipe the tears away.

'I'm sorry. Truly. And if there's still time... I want you to sing. With Mihir. With your full self.'

Priya didn't answer right away. She simply stepped forward and held him—not as a wife returning, but as a woman allowing herself to be seen again.

The silence that followed was not empty. It was sacred.

Devyani smiled. 'Then I'll go now,' she said, rising. 'There's a competition waiting. And a friend who still hasn't selected her song.'

Sunil gave a teary laugh. 'I think I owe someone a phone call.'

Priya looked down, almost shy. 'I think we both do.'

౼౦

The auditorium was packed. Soft murmurs floated through the air as the final name was announced.

Priya stepped onto the stage, her sari anchored, her hands steady. The harmonium sat beside her like a familiar companion. She bowed lightly before taking her seat, her gaze flickering to the front row.

Sunil sat with Sonu on his lap. Devyani was beside them, calm and smiling. Mihir stood just offstage, arms crossed, encouragement shining in his eyes.

Priya closed her eyes for a moment, not to calm her nerves, but to honour the silence that had brought her here—the silence she had lived through, and come out of.

Her first note rose—not the loudest she had ever sung, not the most perfect. But it was alive. Her voice filled the space not with volume, but with presence.

Each note stitched its way through memory and loss, through old doubts and unspoken hopes. By the time she reached the final taan, the air in the hall felt stilled, suspended between her breath and their listening.

When she ended, there was a pause—just a heartbeat—and then the applause began, rising like a wave.

Later, when someone handed her the trophy, she didn't hold it high. She held it close.

She looked through the curtain and found them— Sonu grinning, Sunil standing and clapping, Devyani with her hand over her heart, Mihir smiling quietly.

She stepped back, away from the lights.

Mihir approached. She looked at him for a long moment, then bent and touched his feet. Before he could protest, she said softly, 'Not out of ritual. Out of gratitude.'

He smiled. 'You trusted me. That was enough.'

At that moment, Sunil appeared. He walked up to Mihir and extended his hand. Mihir took it without hesitation. The gesture was quiet, but complete.

As they stepped outside into the night, the drizzle had started again—a faint hush of rain brushing the rooftops. The kind that doesn't soak, only reminds.

They didn't speak. They didn't need to.

Eyes wouldn't fool anymore, and words weren't necessary. Music was about to fill the air.

15

....

Stalked by a Thought

The first flush of the morning is full of glory. The rising sun casts a rosy hue across the sky and the green grass wakes under the shower of dew. Morning walkers soak in the peace of the silent streets.

I wasn't fortunate enough to witness this often. I've always belonged to the late chronotype tribe—pulling away from my cosy pink blanket was a battle. Morning, to me, meant the hours just before noon.

There's an old saying: 'Early to bed and early to rise makes a man healthy, wealthy and wise.' But I had made my peace with the idea that I'd probably be just wise.

Winter is a blessing for people like me. The sun is kinder and the world feels gentler even at 10 a.m. I tied my high ponytail, laced up my white Reeboks and looked at myself in the mirror. I surely looked like a morning walker now. Before stepping out, I dabbed on my sunscreen—a habit picked up long ago to fight my perennial nemesis: tanning.

The park was quiet. Who really walks at 10 a.m.? A pair of lovers were wrapped up in their own world on a bench, teenagers lounged on the grass sharing sandwiches and cigarettes, and two women in faded sari sat in the sun, probably resting after morning chores in someone else's home.

I stopped observing and focused on what I'd come to do—rehearse.

Since childhood, I had a passion for theatre. My father, with his love for poetry, literature and drama, had passed that flame to me. Now, as lead artist in our creative academy's production, I wanted my performance to be flawless. I'd written the prose-poetry myself—it had to flow from me, not just be memorized.

I murmured the lines again and again while pacing the circular path. I must have looked a bit mad, talking to myself—but my crisp clothes and polished face saved me from odd stares. So absorbed was I, I didn't notice the growing dryness in my throat until I was panting.

'You look parched,' said a soft voice.

A woman, seated nearby, was offering me a water bottle. I hesitated. She seemed kind, in her mid-forties, wrapped in a shawl. There was no label on the bottle. She must've seen the hesitation in my eyes.

'It's from home,' she said, smiling gently. 'Safe.'

My throat burned and something about her felt trustworthy. I took it with a quick nod and drank.

'Thank you,' I said, breathing out with relief.

'I hope you don't mind,' she continued, 'but I've been watching you pace and murmur. I couldn't help wondering—what's going on?'

We walked back towards her bench, where a man was seated. He smiled politely. She introduced herself as Reena and added, 'This is my husband, Sameer.'

I explained, 'I'm rehearsing lines. I'm a theatre artist—working on a new piece I wrote.'

'That's fascinating,' Sameer said, leaning in with interest. 'What's it like—becoming a character?'

I smiled. 'It's like being possessed—by something truer than yourself. Sometimes I lose track of where I end and the character begins.'

I paused, then recited a line:

'Why do you think that I need someone to complete me when the human race itself is an incomplete picture? My heart is exposed to vulnerability when I seek for love, but when I look inside, I find it.'

They clapped softly. It was warm and genuine, not exaggerated.

'You've got a gift,' Reena said.

I blushed, shy. 'Thank you.'

The sun had climbed higher. It was time to leave.

As I bid them goodbye and turned around, Sameer called out, 'What's your name?'

'Shriyanka Tripathi' I replied, and left.

The next day slipped past in chores, calls and endless little tasks. By evening, I craved some quiet. I headed to the park again, this time for an evening walk.

But evening was not morning.

The park buzzed—children ran wild, swings creaked, hawkers sold lemon tea and chana jor garam. I missed the stillness of the morning. I slipped in my earphones, letting music drown out the chaos.

Head bowed, I strolled slowly—half-dreaming, half-drifting—when I caught a movement. I looked up.

Sameer.

He was waving. His expression was friendly, but the surprise of seeing him made me freeze in my tracks.

He shouldn't be here. Not again. Not in the crowd. Was he...looking for me?

I panicked. My mind scrambled for a reason, a plan. I turned sharply, pretending not to see him, and walked fast towards the gate. My heart thumped. I didn't wait for my driver, just hailed the nearest rickshaw and gave my address.

Once home, I dropped my bag and stood still, trying to slow my breath. I told myself I was overthinking—but my hands trembled as I poured a glass of water. Why was he there? Was it chance? A coincidence? Or... something else?

Rohit walked in with two cups of tea and paused when he saw me pale and dazed.

'Shri? You okay?'

I took the cup, grateful for the warmth in both the tea and his voice.

'Something happened,' I said. I told him—about the wave, the walk, the man and how I'd run. I tried to keep it matter-of-fact, but I could hear my voice shake.

Rohit listened quietly, then let out a sigh.

'Shri, I love that you trust people. But drinking from a stranger's bottle? Talking freely to someone whose background you don't know?'

I opened my mouth to defend myself, but closed it again. His words stung. But I knew he was right. I'd acted impulsively, and now I didn't know what to believe.

'I won't go back there for a while,' I said. 'Just to be safe.'

He nodded. 'That's wise.'

I touched the chain around my neck absentmindedly. Something felt...lighter. But I was too caught in my thoughts to register what it meant.

❦

Two days passed. The incident in the park had dimmed in the noise of rehearsals and deadlines, though it hadn't vanished completely. After a long practice run, I collapsed on the sofa, my phone in hand. I absentmindedly checked notifications and decided— on a whim—to look through my message requests on Facebook. It was a folder I barely remembered existed.

That's when I saw them. Three messages. From someone named Sameer Kovind. It was him. The man from the park.

My stomach dropped. How had he found me? I hadn't told him my full name, had I? Wait—I had. As I'd left the park that day.

Why was he messaging me? I opened the chat.

Sameer: Hi. I think we crossed paths today. I need to speak with you—it's important.

Sameer: I waved at you today, but maybe you didn't see me or recognize me. Please come to the park tomorrow. I need to give you something.

Sameer: I waited for you to show up, but you didn't. Please let me know how to reach you.

Sameer: Please don't ignore this. It is important.

My fingers stiffened. My stomach turned. The last message was from just a few hours earlier.

I hadn't even seen them—they'd landed in my spam folder, buried out of sight. But now, seeing them all at once, they felt ominous.

I blocked the profile immediately. My palms were sweaty, my throat dry. I wasn't sure whether it was danger or just discomfort. But either way, something in me recoiled.

That night, sleep evaded me. I lay in bed wondering—was I overreacting, or was I not reacting enough?

I woke early the next morning, oddly alert despite the broken sleep. Rohit was still curled up in bed, his breathing soft and even. For a moment, I watched him, envying that peace.

I got up, wrapped my robe around me, and went into the kitchen. The act of brewing tea grounded me.

I turned on the radio, half-humming along to an old tune, trying to distract myself.

Still distracted, I reached for the new ceramic Buddha mugs and rinsed them under the tap. My hand brushed my neck.

I paused. The chain was there—but the pendant was gone.

I frowned, confused. I had worn it just days ago during rehearsal, hadn't I? I tried to trace back the last moment I'd felt its weight, but nothing came.

The doorbell rang. I wasn't expecting anyone. *Probably Sunita,* I thought. My maid didn't have fixed timings and showed up whenever it suited her.

I opened the door and froze. Sameer stood there.

My breath caught. I couldn't speak, couldn't move. My brain tried to plan—grab the vase, shut the door, scream—but nothing came. Fear gripped me like a clamp.

Before I could react, I saw someone in the corridor— Sunita—walking towards the flat. That jolted me back to life.

'Help!' I managed to shout.

Sunita rushed to press the emergency alarm by the lift. In moments, the guard came charging up the stairs, and a few neighbours poked their heads out. The guard lunged forward and grabbed Sameer's arm. Rohit came running from inside.

'Shri! What happened? Are you okay?'

I ran into his arms. 'It's him. The man from the park. He found me on Facebook. Now he's here.'

Sameer, pinned by the guard, shouted, 'Please! I can explain!'

Rohit stepped forward and punched him. 'What the hell are you doing here?'

'Wait,' Sameer said, his breath ragged. 'Just let me say one thing.'

Rohit didn't loosen his grip. Neither did the guard.

'I didn't come to hurt anyone. I'm here to return this.' He gestured to his coat pocket. 'Her pendant. The diamond one. It fell in the park while she was reciting poetry.'

My hand flew to my neck. I gasped.

'You can check my pocket,' he said softly. 'It's there.'

Rohit hesitated, then nodded to the guard. The man reached into Sameer's pocket and drew out a pendant— the same one that had vanished from my neck without me even realizing.

'Why didn't you give it to the police?' Rohit demanded.

'I was worried they wouldn't return it—or that it would get buried in some file. So I waited at the park the next day, hoping to see her. But she avoided me. I tried to find a way to reach her. I remembered her name. Found her online. When she didn't respond, I asked around near the park. Someone at the tea stall knew her driver. That's how I found this place. I swear—I only came to return the pendant.'

Everyone was quiet now.

My mouth was dry. A flush of shame swept over me. In my fear, I'd spun a story. I had imagined threat where there was none. I'd painted a picture of a predator. All from a wave, a message, and a misplaced sense of danger. I had let mistrust blind me.

'I'm so sorry, Sameer,' I said, my voice trembling. 'I should never have assumed. I was afraid—but that doesn't excuse it.'

He nodded. 'I understand. The world doesn't really teach us to trust anymore.'

'Thank you. For going through all this just to return something precious to me.'

As he turned to leave, I felt a strange stillness settle inside me. A quote from Thich Nhat Hanh surfaced in my mind: 'Fear keeps us focused on the past or worried about the future. If we can acknowledge our fear, we can realize that right now we are okay.'

I breathed in. I was okay. And so was the world, for now.

16

Endless Holiday

I believe life is all about finding one's passion. If you live by your passion, then you are truly living.

While watching *Zindagi Na Milegi Dobara* one rainy evening, I couldn't help but think how easily some people 'find' themselves when they go on a holiday—a little pause from the daily grind, a breath of fresh air, a sunset in a foreign land. But for people like us, the opposite is true. To truly find ourselves, we need a break from this endless holiday that life has inadvertently become. We need to return to work, career and priorities.

It's Monday morning. When half the world groans under the weight of Monday blues and the other half charges ahead, geared up for the bustle, there lies Sunanda—our very own Suu—my elder sister. She's sitting on the bed with a tub of popcorn in one hand

and the TV remote in the other. Her pyjamas look worn-in, comfortably familiar, and her oversized T-shirt cheekily declares 'Netflix and Chill'.

I look at her and wonder—could this truly be the same Sunanda I grew up with? Our Suu, the dreamer with her notebook full of poems and doodles. The girl who measured time not in hours but in moments of creativity. The one who searched for meaning in everything—sometimes in raindrops on windowpanes, sometimes in the unspoken words between people. 'Productive' and 'unproductive' were her mantras— even if uniquely defined. She detested wasting time, though her definition of waste was uniquely hers. To Suu, reading a poem she wrote five years ago was more productive than attending a party; learning how to change a car tyre from a friend was more enriching than being chauffeured around by him.

I laughed at her peculiar logic once. But not anymore. I understand it now. She was all about growth— emotional, intellectual, spiritual. She sought meaning in every nook of life, living by a personal philosophy that I admired but never quite grasped until recently.

Today, Suu lives a different life. She's a wife, a pet parent, a hostess to a thriving social circle. Her husband, kind and affectionate, holds a plush corporate job. Their pet, Oreo—a ball of white fluff and mischief— is a Samoyed with the kind of personality that could charm even the grumpiest neighbour. Their apartment is straight out of an issue of *Architectural Digest*—sleek, modern and bathed in warm lighting. She has it all.

Mornings begin with a silver tray carrying bed tea and perfectly scrambled eggs. Her days often revolve around selecting an outfit, planning a lunch date, choosing a dinner place and browsing the latest collections in luxury boutiques. Every detail of her life appears curated, seamless, spotless.

Anyone who doesn't know Suu might envy her life. 'She's got it all,' they would say. Comfort. Stability. Joy. A dream come true.

But I knew better.

I've been here only a week in 'Dilwalon ki Dilli' and I already feel the burn of monotony from endless city tours, shopping hauls, dining at India's most elite fine-dining spots and mingling with her friends who all looked like they have walked out of fashion campaigns.

I finally blurt out, 'How are you doing this?'

'Doing what?' she asks.

'This...this routine of nothingness! Doesn't it bore you?'

She chuckles, lifting her tea cup. 'No. In fact, I'm loving it. My life's all about "Eat, Pray, Love" now.'

'Come on, Suu. Life was never just about "Eat, Pray, Love". Not for you, at least.'

Her eyes soften. 'Oh, but now it is. I never knew such a life existed—no deadlines, no fear. Just calm, comfort and pleasure.'

But I remembered a different Suu.

↶

Suu was once an intern at a buzzing news channel in Ludhiana. She wanted to be the next Barkha Dutt. Her charm, her insights, her voice—all screamed journalism. She was articulate, informed, fearless. She was made for the field and the field knew it.

I remember when she ventured into Ludhiana's red-light district for a story. People warned her not to. But Suu wasn't one to listen to fear. She wrote a ground-shaking piece titled 'The Forbidden Area That Bleeds Red', capturing the stories of women whose lives had been reduced to shadows. The article made waves. She was invited on panels, featured in newspapers and awarded the Regional Press Freedom Award. Suu was suddenly the name on everyone's lips—the Jugni of Ludhiana.

One blazing summer, she wore her favourite bright yellow kurti with a swirling orange dupatta and silver jhumkas that jingled with every step. She looked radiant, alive, like a flame dancing in daylight.

'I've got to look like sunshine,' she had said. 'I'm interviewing the mayor today.'

'You look more like a traffic signal,' I joked and she burst out laughing.

Mum came running with her spoon of curd and jaggery. She even added a black dot of kajal behind Suu's ear to protect her from the evil eye.

The mayor arrived late as expected, but the interview had gone smoothly. Suu was in her element, firing questions with the confidence of a veteran. After the session, the mayor invited her to the press club for a cup of tea.

After a hectic day, Suu needed tea, so she agreed. *It's just tea*, she'd thought.

The garden at the club was quiet. They sat across a small round table draped in white satin. The afternoon was hot and humid, so not many people were around.

They were served piping hot ginger tea and freshly baked buns—almost too fresh for an afternoon tea. It made Suu wonder—had these been specially baked for him?

The mayor, in his early forties with a mix of grey and black in his hair and moustache, looked at her with interest. They discussed journalism and politics as a single waiter paced nearby.

Mayor Aminder leaned forward, his voice soft. 'What challenges do you face as a woman in this field?' he asked.

Suu felt hope. *Finally*, she thought, *someone who acknowledges the struggle.*

She opened up, passionately explaining how hard it was to be taken seriously as a woman journalist, how people questioned her capability, how her parents worried for her safety every single day. 'It's tough... A constant negotiation between fear and drive.'

He stared at her as she spoke, nodding along and giving her a reassuring smile.

'Must be exhausting,' he murmured.

And then, without warning, he grabbed her hand.

Startled, she froze, not knowing how to react.

'I want to see you tonight. Golden Hotel. Sharp

at nine,' he said, as though placing an order at a restaurant.

She yanked her hand away, stunned.

'I can solve all your problems,' he continued, his voice now dripping with threat cloaked as kindness. 'My bed could be your ticket to success.'

Her breath caught in her throat. And then, with the force of a storm gathering for years, she slapped him hard across the face.

The sound echoed. Through the garden. Through her very being.

Shocked, he stood up, his face flushed with humiliation and rage. 'You slapped the mayor? I'll ruin you! I have the power. I'll get you framed. I'll destroy your name! You'll be labelled an extortionist by morning.'

The mayor stormed off. Suu felt numb. Her body refused to move. Her mind raced with images of shame, disgrace, injustice. He was right—he had the power to wreck her. She was a girl from a simple middle-class family, standing alone before a political Goliath. She thought about her parents—they would be so ashamed and embarrassed. A single tear rolled down her cheek. The black dot hadn't protected her.

But then something shifted. I am not a coward.

She wiped her tears, pulled out her phone and made a call to her friend at the channel. She briefly explained the situation, asked for support and then began calling every press contact she knew.

Within ten minutes, the press club teemed with reporters. Tripods, mics, buzzing questions. A makeshift press conference began in the hall. Suu stood before them, her voice unwavering.

As the mayor emerged from the restroom, wiping his face, he noticed the gathering.

'What's going on?' he barked at the waiter.

'Ji, aaj sherni di conference si, the lioness is holding a conference,' the waiter replied with a smirk.

Before the mayor could utter another word, police officers surrounded him. 'You're under arrest under Section 354A of the IPC,' they declared.

He screamed, 'On what basis?'

'For the sexual harassment of Miss Sunanda Verma,' replied one of the officers.

'You can't arrest the mayor on a woman's word!' he screamed. 'Where is your proof?'

The officer calmly responded, 'We have a video recorded by a waiter. It's all there. The video's gone viral.'

Suu came to stand in front of the mayor, unyielding, her gaze piercing through him. The power he once wielded crumbled.

The legal battle that followed was long, draining and brutal. The courtroom echoed with accusations. Threats were made. Her character was attacked. But Suu never bowed down. She endured. And in the end, she won.

She received awards. Standing ovations. Invitations to speak at forums. She became an inspiration for the women and girls of the city. Whenever she took to the mic, she never failed to mention 'God helps those who help themselves'.

But behind all that applause was a woman who had fought every step of the way. A woman who had lost a part of herself in the process.

⌒

The smell of freshly brewed tea tugs me back to the present. Suu hands me a cup of ginger cardamom tea. I look at the other glass in her hand.

'Still drinking tea in your lassi glass?' I ask, laughing.

'Toh aur kya? Sikhni hun main Bhatinda ki, what else? I'm a Sikhni from Bhatinda!' she replies, mimicking Geet from *Jab We Met*, the same twinkle in her eyes from years ago.

That laugh—that unfiltered, spontaneous laughter—was the first time I have heard it in years. And in that moment, I understand. Behind the carefree facade is a woman who has been to hell and back. Who has lost her innocence but never her soul.

The fight broke her in ways only time could heal. Even after victory, the whispers lingered, the scars remained. She gave up the mic, the spotlight, the bylines—not out of defeat, but because she had earned her stillness.

She deserves this peace. She has earned her rest. Who am I to question her joy?

We are conditioned to measure success in milestones, not in healing. But healing is the greatest victory. And for Suu, this endless holiday called life is nothing short of a triumph.

Acknowledgements

With each step in life, I have come to realize a simple truth—I am not the doer. I am deeply grateful to the divine power—my God and this benevolent universe—for allowing this work to take shape. It has been nothing short of magical, each page finding its place in its own perfect, divine timing. I am forever thankful to the Almighty for making it all possible.

To my husband, Rohit—my mentor, my partner and my guide—my heart overflows with love and gratitude. You have been the first listener of every story, hearing them fresh from the page. You stayed awake with me in the quiet hours of the night simply to keep me company while I wrote. Your encouragement, your faith in me and your honest feedback have been priceless. You are truly a blessing in my life—the one who believed in the writer within me, even before I recognized her myself.

To my parents, who raised me differently—instilling in me belief and confidence—thank you for your blessings and guidance. To my in-laws, thank you for your constant support.

I am grateful to my little sunshine, Vivaan, who has been the most excited for this book and is always proud of whatever his mumma does.

My heartfelt thanks to everyone at Rupa Publications— this book would not have been possible without your support.

And finally, to my readers—thank you for choosing my work, giving these stories a home in your hearts and making me a writer.